Bloody Mary, Bloody Murder

Tanya Westlake

Impractical Press

Chapter One

"Can you believe that fight on the beach tonight?"

"That was so crazy! Don't these people know they're supposed to be having *fun*?"

"And their friends all stood around recording it. How embarrassing. It's probably up on social media already!"

Kallie Brooks finished cleaning the bar as she listened to her friends talk about the latest Spring Break madness. She carefully moved the boxes of napkins back to their places under the counter and corralled the last dirty glasses in the washing rack for the kitchen guys to pick up later.

The gossip grew louder as the speakers neared the front door, and Kallie's colleagues called out a tired but cheerful goodnight to her. She looked up as Mike locked the front door behind Melanie, and the conversation stopped. Melanie's boyfriend, waiting outside for her, waved goodnight as they walked to his car at the curb. The young blonde waitress was still chattering and moving her hands animatedly, as she apparently told her boyfriend all about her night. *Exuberant as always*, Kallie thought with a smile.

Melanie disappeared into the passenger seat of their car, still talking.

As Mike walked back to the office, cracking his neck tiredly on the way, she carried the till out to a table to close it out. Their wild young customers were all gone, leaving only five of them in the quiet bar – Mike and Kallie, plus their boss, the night manager, and one other bartender – closing up for the night.

Wiping the sticky residue of sugary drinks off one side of a table, Kallie sat down and took off her shoes. The boss wouldn't let most of the employees handle the whole register unattended, but Kallie had been working here for six years and Marcy trusted her. Besides, she could add up the totals without resorting to using the calculator on her phone – or counting on her fingers and toes, like Tony, the new guy. The college girls loved Tony, but he wasn't the sharpest knife in the drawer.

She piled the few checks and many curled-up credit card receipts next to the cash, along with the tabs. As she tallied them all up easily in her small notebook, she thought back to the call from her mom that morning, expressing her worry over Kallie's brother. She had been having trouble reaching him and said she was worried that he might be in trouble again.

But she didn't have time to think about it now, especially since her brother was *always* in trouble, so she pushed it to the back of her mind. She finished her accounting, separated the tips from the tabs, and pocketed her own take for the night. Not a bad evening, even if it meant dealing with a few more drunken fraternity boys than usual. At least they were *rich* frat boys, whose parents had apparently taught them the nearly lost art of tipping. And tipping well, if you plan to visit again. Their generosity would cover the rest of her bills for the month.

Slipping her shoes back on, and wincing as they pinched her swollen, tired feet, she carried the two stacks back to the office. Marcy looked up and smiled as she opened the door. "Done for the night, Kal?"

"Yes, ma'am," Kallie replied with a tired smile at her boss and longtime friend. "It's going to be an early morning."

"I don't know how you have the energy to volunteer on Sunday mornings after spending Saturday nights here. You know I stay in bed until noon, right?"

She was kidding, of course. Marcy was an early morning jogger and often ran three miles before most people had even thought about eating breakfast. Kallie had never seen her sleep and suspected she was secretly a robot — but if so, she was a nice one.

"It keeps me humble," she replied with a laugh. "Besides, I need the good karma after dealing with these kids all night. Tell me again, when is Spring Break over?"

"Around July, I think. It gets longer every year."

Kallie put the night's take in a zippered envelope and slipped it into the safe, waving goodnight as Marcy went back to her ledger. Just outside the office, Carlos was standing by the back door, waiting to walk her out to her car. The parking lot was well-lit, and they weren't in a bad neighborhood, but they didn't take any chances. The bar's safety measures had seemed silly to her when she started, but after a local serial killer had terrorized another part of Tampa Bay a few years ago, she now welcomed the company on her way out.

Mike, the remaining security guard, was waiting for Marcy. She could see that he was armed, since they'd need to stop at the bank. Neither of the guys would let Kallie walk out alone anyway, even if she insisted on it. In the time she'd been there, they had both become like very large, very protective, big brothers to her. Carlos, the Lazy Gecko's night shift floor manager, was not only one of the smartest people Kallie knew, he was also easily one of the biggest. Built like an oak tree, he'd tear the arms off of anyone who even thought of hurting her. To her, though, he was a giant teddy bear.

The warm and muggy night air hit them like a brick wall as they walked outside, even though it was only late March. For now, she was grateful that the tropical humidity took the chill off her skin after the permanently arctic air conditioning of the bar. They walked quietly to her car, with Carlos keeping an eye out for any lurking dangers.

"Oh, hey, I'm almost finished with that blanket,"

Kallie broke the silence. "Let me know if you pick a name, and I can add it."

Carlos's wife was pregnant with their first kid, a girl, and she had been on prescribed bed rest for over two months. They were both pretty nervous, but her due date was now only about a week away. Kallie was knitting a fluffy pink baby blanket. "I can bring over more food, too, since I know you're not going to cook." She nudged him with her elbow, and he laughed self-consciously.

"I can cook, Kallie. I can make toast, and Kraft Mac and Cheese, and... ice?"

"I'll make some lasagna or baked ziti or something. They say marinara sauce helps kick-start labor."

"That sounds amazing. For both reasons. I'll let Isabel know. And maybe it'll help convince her to stay in bed."

Isabel was an exercise instructor with her own small but very popular studio, and Kallie knew the isolation and stillness were driving her nuts. She had two employees that were keeping the business going strong, but staying in bed was almost impossible for her. She had barely tolerated it at first, but knew it was important to keep the baby healthy. Now that she was basically full-term, Kallie was sure she'd be running a marathon with her giant baby belly, if Carlos didn't keep the doors locked.

Beneath the shadowing trees in the back row of the bar's parking lot, he bent down to check under her car with his flashlight and even glanced into the back seat suspiciously. Finally, he nodded that she could unlock the door. She thought it was silly but kept her mouth shut, glad to have a protector of her own for once.

They waved goodnight as Kallie got into her car, and Carlos walked back to the bar.

Starting the car and putting it into reverse, she instinctively grabbed the broken rearview mirror and adjusted it to make sure no one was behind her, and then laughed at herself. *Behind me at 3:00 a.m.? In a deserted parking lot?* She shook her head and let go of the dangling mirror, but something caught her eye as it dropped.

Suddenly wide awake, Kallie lifted the mirror and looked out the back window again. *What did I just see?*

There was nothing, now. Maybe it had been cross traffic on the mostly empty road behind the bar, or one of those huge local ducks flying past. She dropped the mirror again, but paused, unconvinced. *There was something... What did I see?* Trusting her gut, she physically turned in the driver's seat for one last look.

There it was. Something on the back seat, on the passenger side. Had she left a water bottle or something back there? It was too dark to see. Anyway, she could check when she got home. She started to pull out of the parking space again, but something stopped her. Feeling foolish, and yet trusting both her well-engrained instincts and the chill running up her back, she turned off the car and got out. She opened the back door, expecting to find a folded-up shopping bag or one of her Converse shoes.

It was too dark, and the dome light in the back seat wasn't working either. Feeling alone and exposed outside in the dark, she quickly dug in her purse for her phone, hands shaking just a little. After taking a deep breath, she turned on the screen flashlight, and then held it out, leaning into the car to see.

Kallie suddenly stifled a scream, backpedaling away from the car. Whipping around, she searched for Carlos, but he was already inside the bar. She quickly reached through the front door again, scrambling with her hands below the dashboard. Her father always made sure she had it when she was going on trips, and she knew it was still there. *Come on!* Her fingers closed around the can of pepper spray, and she ripped it from the built-in holder. There was a red and white umbrella propped against the front passenger seat, and she leaned over to grab that too.

Fighting panic, she stood up and returned to the back door. "GET OUT! Get out, get out! *NOW!*" she yelled.

The shadowed hand in her back seat didn't move.

She smashed the seat cushions with the umbrella, and banged her fist on the metal roof, to make more noise, but there was still no movement.

They must have heard her from inside the bar, because Carlos and Mike were both coming her way now, fast. She backed away from the car, keeping the pepper spray aimed at the back seat. As they ran over, Mike drew his own weapon, and Carlos quickly pulled her away.

"What is it, Kallie?"

"There's... I saw someone in my back seat. I tried to get them to move, but..."

"Carlos?" Mike asked, "Didn't you—"

"I checked the back seat. Are you sure—"

But by then Mike had pulled out his own security flashlight.

"STEP OUT OF THE CAR!" he roared suddenly.

He ran around to the passenger side and tore open the rear door, reaching in to roughly pull out the hiding invader. Carlos sheltered Kallie, and he was already on the phone with the police.

Kallie couldn't see what Mike was doing on the other side of her car, but his voice and demeanor suddenly became less aggressive.

"Come on now, lady, this isn't your car. We'll get

you a taxi and you can sleep it off at home," he continued, much more quietly. "Get out before the cops get here and make it worse."

As he reached down to pull gently on the mysterious wrist, he finally froze. Jerking his hand away, he blinked like someone just waking up from a strange dream, and he met Kallie's eyes over the top of the car.

"Oh, Kallie. I'm sorry, we need to wait for the cops. I'm pretty sure she's dead."

* * * * *

One of the local Owhiro cops was talking to Marcy about the security camera feeds, while the other met with the paramedics. Both had been kind and patient with Kallie and said they'd need to ask where she'd been all evening, but the security and forensic questions were more pressing.

A very serious-looking detective had stayed outside with Mike to get his firsthand story about the body, and another walked her and Carlos back inside, talking about the 911 call. Separating them in different rooms, he asked politely that they stick around for questioning.

The smallest table in the Lazy Gecko's VIP lounge seated eight, so Kallie chose that one to sit and wait after the detective had shepherded her into the room.

And now she *was* just sitting and waiting, for what seemed like an hour. She felt like a little kid, left all alone at this awkwardly huge table. She took a bag of gummy bears out of her purse and nervously ate a few. Her shoes were once again abandoned on the floor, and she had pulled her tired feet up onto the seat until she was almost in an upright fetal position.

When Mike told her that the hidden person was probably dead, Carlos had immediately pulled Kallie farther away to his own car, sheltering her, so she hadn't even really seen anything. Only that terrifying hand. She wasn't sure what – if anything – she would be able to tell the police when they came back for her. *They're going to think you're lying*, she thought nervously. *They'll think it's your fault. Try to remember something.*

The car doors had been locked — she was meticulous about that — but it would be pretty easy to force open an old car like hers. And she never turned on the alarm anymore because the clicker to turn it off stopped working about a year ago. Besides, there were hired security guards outside, watching the parking lot. *Yeah, that awesome security team managed to miss a dead body, so maybe I'll start turning on the alarm again.*

The parking lot was always unusually crowded

this time of year because of Spring Break, so employees had to park in the back row for about a month. It had never bothered any of them, but Kallie thought Marcy would now change that policy pretty quickly.

"Miss Brooks? Sorry to keep you waiting," one of the detectives shook her out of her reflection. She sat up straighter and started to put her shoes back on, but then decided he could cope with her bare feet.

"No problem," she replied, trying to force a smile. "It's not like I'll be able to sleep when I get home. I might as well be here."

Sitting down on the opposite side of the oval table, the detective pulled out an old-fashioned notepad and pen. He seemed unusually scruffy for a cop, she thought, with a slightly wrinkled shirt and much more than a five o'clock shadow. *That's because it's past three a.m., silly. He's probably been working for at least ten hours straight.* His badge said he was from St Petersburg, which was twenty miles away, at the southern end of the county.

"I'm Detective Morrison. I've spoken to your friends, but I need you to tell me in your own words what happened. Can you start from when you arrived tonight?"

Kallie described her arrival at the Lazy Gecko a little before seven that evening, and she told him she'd had a hard time finding a spot in the back row.

"The college kids had apparently been camped

out drinking ever since the bar opened this morning," she explained. "So I had to make a few loops before I could find a parking place. I don't usually park under the oak trees in the back corner of the lot, you know. I prefer a spot where the car's visible from the doorway, but that's all I could find."

The detective nodded but didn't look up from his notebook.

"And I made sure it was locked," she told him. "It may not be a new car, but I like it. I always make sure it's locked." Kallie realized she sounded defensive, but she didn't want him to think she was a flake.

"Oh, we know it was locked," he nodded. "Someone forced the rear passenger side lock with a screwdriver. Not sure yet if it was the killer, or possibly the victim or someone else, but hopefully we'll be able to find out from the security footage."

"Victim? Wait, *killer?*"

The detective remained silent, which she found a little unnerving. She kept talking to fill the awkwardly quiet space.

"Mike said— He thought it was a woman. He was talking to her like she was drunk. I guess I thought someone just climbed into the wrong car and passed out. And then... overdosed or something. Wow." She stared at her hands on the table in shock for another minute in the lengthening silence. "Can you tell me what happened? I didn't really see anything after I jumped out of the car. "

"The crime scene team will determine more of the details. The body hasn't been removed yet, but yes, it appears to be a woman. Small stature. We'll be asking whether you know her once they get some photos, but for now, we only know she's petite and blonde. Small enough to fit into the leg space of your backseat."

It suddenly clicked.

"Wait, somebody crammed her *whole body* into that tiny space? That's why I could only see her hand? That's... crazy. That's horrible." She shook her head, overwhelmed, trying to come up with better words. Trying to wake up from this nightmare.

"There will probably be additional trauma from the method of hiding the body," he replied noncommittally, keeping an emotional distance from the gruesome details. "Again, the crime scene technicians will need to confirm that."

"It wasn't one of the customers, was it? With a pissed-off boyfriend or something?"

"We don't know yet, but no, it doesn't appear to be a patron of the bar. At least not a tourist."

He tried to change the subject, and she let him. She didn't want to think about the logistics of getting a grown woman, even a small one, into a space that size. Her mind would surely keep her up all night with the gory details, and that could wait.

"You mentioned overdosing. Is there a lot of drug use at the bar?"

"Not normally, no. Marcy wouldn't tolerate it. But with so many out-of-towners on vacation, in such a packed crowd, it's hard to tell what changes hands."

The detective nodded silently again, taking notes. "Could you continue with the timeline of your night? Did you go back outside at all after you arrived? Did you see anything suspicious or odd?"

"No, it's Spring Break — well, you know that — so we were packed to capacity all night. There was no chance to step away, even for a bite to eat. And as for suspicious, nothing's weird when you have a ton of drunk college kids in town. There was a couple dressed as Mr. and Mrs. Disco Shark from that cartoon, except all in real-life glitter and spandex. There were three guys zip-tied together at the wrist, which I think was some kind of fraternity thing. A lot of underdressed girls. A few angry scuffles about spilled beers, but certainly nothing that seemed violent or dangerous."

Kallie's pulse began to slow a little as she talked to the detective, and he wrote down all of her details, asking a few questions but mostly listening. It was calming to talk about the mundane details, as if they mattered, and forget about the dead body in her car for a few minutes.

* * * * *

The police needed to keep her car as evidence, so Mike offered to drive Kallie home and told her he'd take her to get a rental car in the morning. She lived in the opposite direction from his home, but he didn't complain at all as he drove – he was more occupied with watching for any threats in the dark.

"Do you want me to walk you to the door, Kal?" he asked, putting the car in park outside her house.

If anyone else asked, she'd think they were flirting. She and Mike had known each other for years, though, and he'd always looked out for her like this.

"I come home every night, Mike," she smiled. "I'm fine. No one's following me."

He looked like he was going to argue, but finally agreed to just watch carefully until she got inside. She hugged him goodnight and thanked him again, and then took out her house keys and showed him that she remembered how to stick them between her fingers like a weapon.

"Good girl," he nodded with a worried smile.

The path to the front door was well-lit, and Kallie approached cautiously but safely. Unlocking the door quietly, she listened for a minute before she walked inside, waving at Mike to let him know he could go.

"Good evening, roomie," a voice called from the

shadows. "Although it's almost good morning."

"Dad! I'm so sorry, I was trying to be quiet." Even with her late hours at work, she was usually home by three a.m. — tonight she was much later.

"Marcy called me, sweetheart. She didn't want me to worry. Are you okay?"

She started to nod, but knew her father would call her out on the lie. "Not really."

"Want to talk about it?"

"Not really," she replied again, with a crooked smile. "Not yet."

"That's okay. I'm here if you change your mind. And I made you hot chocolate and toast."

Her favorite midnight snack, even though it was long past midnight. "Thanks, Dad." Her eyes started to tear up, and he pretended not to notice.

"They're probably still warm, if you hurry," he told her gently.

"Is it Wonder Bread toast?" she asked with a laugh.

"Of course it is. Have I ever let you down?"

Chapter Two

When Tess Russo arrived to pick up her best friend for volunteering at the local food kitchen at 7 a.m., Kallie had only managed to doze off for about ten minutes. That was enough. She'd woken up in a cold sweat around 5:30 a.m., jumping at her own dreaming yelp — and waking Sherman, her rescued border collie mix, in the process. He leaned over to lick her ear, then quickly went back to sleep, but Kallie was done.

Never sleeping again, she promised herself, trying to forget the sea of young, blonde, faceless nightmare girls begging for her help in the dream. *Never.*

Crawling out of bed, she had crept quietly to the kitchen and started a big pot of coffee, then threw on some sweatpants to go with her nightshirt and walked to the newspaper dispenser on the corner. It was a safe neighborhood, even in the pre-dawn darkness, but she pitied any criminal with the poor timing to bother her in this current mood. She and the local paper made it home unscathed, and she read the sports and comics sections — and drank *all* of the coffee — carefully avoiding the crime section.

There would be plenty of time for facing the

issue later, but the dream had shaken her up more than she liked to admit, and she needed to keep herself together right now. Her father and best friend would be glad to help her, but she needed to put on a brave face and get through the morning.

After starting another pot of coffee at six, stronger this time and dosed with cinnamon, she had taken a quick shower, but she found herself suddenly nervous about being so exposed and alone. She'd never had that feeling in this house, where she'd lived for so long, even before her dad moved back in.

Kallie tried to wash off the fear-sweat stench that still seemed to permeate all the way to the roots of her hair, but couldn't shake the sense of alarm. Giving up, she towel-dried her shoulder-length dark auburn hair and tossed on a pair of comfortable jeans and a t-shirt covered in cartoonish pastel manatees. *Nothing cheers a girl up like a lavender sea potato.*

Checking the mirror, the dark circles under her olive-green eyes were a dead giveaway that she hadn't slept. She didn't usually wear makeup to volunteer, but she swiped on a little mascara and a ton of concealer to avoid questions.

Tess knocked on the front door just as Kallie was tying her shoes, and her heart jumped with relief. She filled her travel mug with the rest of the coffee and about a pound of sugar, then ran for the door.

It had only been a few days since they'd seen

each other, but she fell into Tess's hug like it was the only safety line that might save her from drowning.

Her friend obviously hadn't heard the news yet, since it had barely been four hours, but she immediately knew something was wrong. She finally broke their embrace and looked Kallie in the face, lifting her chin.

"Hey, what's wrong?"

Kallie shook her head, still not ready to talk.

Looking at the barely-concealed dark circles under her eyes, she asked, "Have you even slept? Wait, it's not your dad, right?!"

Kallie shook her head again. "No, no. Dad's fine. And no, I haven't slept," she added with an embarrassed smile. "Let's just go, okay?"

Tess sighed, but Kallie knew she'd let it wait for the moment. "Okay, let's go. You'll feel better when we get to the outreach center and Mack starts flirting with you."

Mack was an adorable man of about eighty, whose deceased wife had apparently looked quite a bit like Kallie. He called her Francesca Maria and always insisted that Kallie swing dance with him at least twice on Sunday mornings at the center before church services started. She sometimes even practiced new steps in her spare time.

"Everything's right with the world when Mack's dancing, Tess," she replied, trying to sound cheerful and failing. "I'll tell you about it later."

"Okay, okay," her best friend agreed. "Hey, where's your car?"

"*Later*," Kallie sighed again.

* * * * *

The smell of fresh soup at the food kitchen hit Kallie in the face as she and her best friend walked through the back door, and the scent set her stomach growling immediately. *Brilliant, two pots of coffee and no food. Great planning.*

They served both breakfast and lunch on Sundays, even though it was only barely light outside, since there was a church service in the attached shelter. This kept them open longer than usual, and patrons could grab a meal both before and after if they wanted. Chefs from a few of the local four- and five-star restaurants volunteered for this well-run charity organization, and the food was always amazing. The staff carried out a huge tray of yeast rolls, and Kallie's stomach protested even louder.

Knowing the day would be too hot for soup when their shift was over, and wishing she'd thought to eat breakfast, Kallie asked for a small cup. The waffles, sausage, and eggs were always the most popular dishes anyway, so she didn't feel too bad. Kallie and Tess volunteered almost every week, so the chef handed over a full bowl of his best chicken and wild rice soup with only some minor teasing. It was as delicious as it smelled, and it heartily braced Kallie for her serving duties.

Fed and cheered up by the familiar faces in line, she was happy to be able to take her mind off the previous night for a little while. A few employees from the shelter, who must have seen the morning news, came over and hugged her, but they were kind enough to leave it at that. They couldn't have known the details, but they knew where she worked – knew she must've been there – and probably felt her stress. This was a place of privacy and empathy, and that extended to the volunteers.

"Francesca Maria!" her old friend called to her. "Beautiful girl, what are you doing in this hot kitchen?"

"Oh, Mack," she grinned. "Don't you know I just came to bring you some breakfast? Will it be pancakes and bacon, my dear? Your favorite? With black coffee?"

He accepted his plate with a chivalrous bow and salsa'ed off to sit with his friends.

"He'll be back for that dance, you know," Tess whispered to Kallie.

"I hope so! I've been practicing the Lindy Hop since Wednesday. I found a video online." She waggled her feet and swung her hips. "I just hope I don't step on his toes."

Tess watched Kallie's feet and whistled. "You're getting pretty good at this stuff, girl."

"I was practicing with a chair, so let's hold off on the compliments until we see how many paramedics are involved."

Tess laughed and elbowed her in the ribs. "Hush, you. You're going to make his day!"

They quickly went back to serving breakfast as the crowds picked up. The line was longer than usual since the building had air conditioning. In June the rainy season would start, and the mornings would be cool again, but right now they were lucky to get below eighty degrees overnight. Almost everyone took coffee, but there were also dozens of pitchers of ice water on the tables. Many folks had water bottles of various sizes and qualities, and they refilled them all carefully. It was going to be another hot day on the streets.

* * * * *

After breakfast and chatting, and watching a little dancing, most of the patrons went to the church service. Kallie and Tess and the other volunteers cleaned up the tables and packaged the rest of the breakfast food into bundles to go. Many would stay for soup and sandwiches after the service, and they would have stomachs full for the day. Some of the packets could be traded, though, or given away to more introverted friends who disliked the crowded food kitchen.

The chefs packed up their giant soup pots and mixing bowls after everything was doled out, and the permanent employees hugged everyone goodbye with more thanks. Kallie came here because she loved the place and believed in their work in the community, but the hugs and thanks helped too. Especially on a day like this, when her stress was starting to wash back in with reality.

As they walked back to the car, Kallie could sense Tess looking at her. "I can see you tensing up again already. Are you sure you don't want to talk about it?"

She hugged her friend with one arm as they walked the last few steps to the car. When they got in, Kallie turned on the air conditioning, turned off the radio, and told Tess the whole thing. The night, the college kids, Marcy, the dark parking lot. The hand. *The horrible little hand in the shadows*. And then Mike and Carlos and the police and the paramedics and the fancy VIP table with the detective where she felt so small and helpless.

Tess sat in silence and listened, only nodding, and let her finish. In the end, she hugged her best friend tightly across the center console, and Kallie broke into sobs against her shoulder. For the first time breaking down in her fear and horror and sadness. At her thought of that poor unknown girl reduced to nothing. At the loss of her own sense of unshakeable safety in her hometown, where she had never worried about walking at night. At all of it and nothing.

After she had settled down, Tess asked, "Do you want to get the newspapers and read them at my house? Or watch the local news? Or do you want to go watch that new Pixar movie and forget all about it?"

Kallie laughed and wiped off the last of her tear-streaked mascara in the mirror. "How about both?"

"You got it, babe."

"And can we stop at Taco Bus?"

"Oh, I think we're stopping at both Taco Bus *and* Dairy Queen this time."

Chapter Three

After stopping at Publix to buy *all* of the local newspapers from both sides of the Bay — and then a detour for ice cream, horchata, and the best tacos in town — they returned to Tess's house and turned on the local 24-hour news station. On the weekends, the pre-recorded news stories ran in hour-long loops, with highlights on the half hour, so they knew they wouldn't need to watch for long.

Within fifteen minutes, the story was mentioned, but they were both surprised at how little was covered. A woman had been found deceased outside the popular Lazy Gecko bar in Owhiro at closing time, and police were investigating and asking for witnesses to come forward. Nothing about the car, or the state of the body. No name of the victim. The anchor at the desk didn't even cut to a recording of a reporter at the scene.

"That was short," Kallie complained.

"I guess the police need to keep some of the information out of the press, since only the killer would know those details?" Tess didn't sound convinced at her own suggestion.

"They didn't even mention that she was murdered. They made it sound like she just... died. And they didn't say the victim's name."

"They have to notify the next of kin before they can announce it on the news. I know that much," Tess explained. "That way the family doesn't hear about it first on TV."

"That would be awful," Kallie nodded. "Maybe she was from out of town and they haven't found her family yet. The detective said he didn't think she was a college student on Spring Break, though. He thought she was a local."

"Lots of locals don't have any family in town, though. Even I don't anymore."

Tess had family in Georgia, but Kallie knew it wouldn't take twelve hours to get an emergency message to them. "The detective gave me his card," she remembered, digging in her purse to find it. "He told me to call if I remembered anything. I wonder if I can ask *him* questions?"

Now that she was talking with Tess and had gotten her emotions out, her natural curiosity was kicking in. She suddenly wanted to know more. *Why is there nothing on the news? Every other murder in town immediately becomes the lead story.*

"Hmm, I doubt he could tell you her name or anything," Tess replied hesitantly. "Let's check the newspapers first, and look online. There are some local bloggers who pick up the news and do their own research. Especially on crime."

They each took a newspaper and read them cover to cover while they finished off their tacos and started on caramel sundaes, but the papers had even less information than the TV news. Searching online was a little better. Kallie was shocked to see that someone had taken a picture of her car, with the back doors still standing wide open, and posted it on a blog. There were a dozen photos of the police and the ambulance at the bar, bedecked in crime scene tape. *Who could have snuck into the parking lot at 3:00 a.m. and taken pictures without being stopped by the police?*

Still no name of the victim or details on the blog.

After an hour they gave up, and Tess could see that Kallie was starting to get shaky and stressed again, so she called it off. "Still up for that new movie?"

"Yep," Kallie replied immediately, snapping the laptop shut and stuffing her newspaper into the recycle bin.

"I hear it has talking koalas."

"Sold. Let's go."

* * * * *

"Hi Mister Brooks," Tess called out when they

27

returned to Kallie's house. Kallie bought the house from her parents when they split up, not wanting it to be sold, and lived there alone for ten years before her father moved back in. He had been living alone too, and she didn't want to wait until his health started failing. Besides, he made a great roommate — quiet, considerate, funny, and he didn't nag her about occasionally eating Wonder Bread.

"Hi, Tess!" He'd been tinkering with the scroll saw in the garage, creating a flamingo from a small sheet of wood, and walked back inside to greet them. "Have you had lunch? I can fix you something."

"We've eaten, Mister B."

He nodded agreeably. "Kallie, the detective came by and asked for you. He said he had some more questions, and I told him I'd have you call him back."

"Did he say anything about my car?"

"No, but I didn't think to ask. Wasn't your friend Mike going to take you to get a rental today?"

"I was hoping I wouldn't need it." Kallie took the note from her dad and dialed the detective's number on her cell, pausing to take a deep breath before hitting the last number. The angry butterflies in her stomach woke back up as she dreaded talking about the murder again.

She thought about going outside on the patio to make the call, but then realized it might be better for the others to hear the conversation. They'd probably have helpful questions. She sat down at the dining room table instead, and put the phone on speaker.

Detective Morrison answered his phone on the third ring.

"Hi Detective. It's Kalliope Brooks, returning your call."

"Hi, Miss Brooks, thanks for calling me back. I have a few more questions for you. Would it be okay if I swing by your house later?"

"Oh, sure," Kallie replied. "I wasn't expecting you to come back up to Owhiro, but that would be a lot more convenient."

"Yeah, since we still have your car."

"Exactly."

"Since it's the primary crime scene, so far, it will probably take a few more days to process."

"Okay, then I'll definitely need to run out and get a rental car." She nodded at her dad. "I don't want to rely on everyone else, since I work late hours."

"If I plan to get there at six o'clock, will that give you enough time?"

Kallie agreed that six should be fine, and they hung up. There was a small car rental company nearby that she had used once before, so she knew they accepted her insurance. It shouldn't take too long as long as they had cars available. She figured the Spring Break crowd mostly rented their cars at the airport, but she'd check their inventory and make sure.

With perfect timing, Mike texted her five minutes later and asked if she still needed a ride, telling her he'd be there in fifteen minutes.

* * * * *

"I was thinking I might go in to work after we pick up the rental car. It seems silly to have it and not use it." *And it beats sitting at home crying and feeling like I suddenly have a target on my back,* she thought to herself.

"Isn't it your night off?" Mike asked. He'd come inside to visit for a minute while Kallie gathered her insurance paperwork.

"Yes, but—"

He shook his head. "Marcy isn't expecting you, Kal. I mean, if you want to go talk to her, that's one thing. But you can't work tonight. Seriously, if you try to work a shift, she'll kill me."

"I'd rather be working than—"

"Nope. I think she's even more shaken up about this than you are. If I let you go to work, she will literally feed me to an alligator."

"When she called last night," Kallie's father added, "she mentioned that she didn't really want you working nights for a while. She was planning to put you on the afternoon shift and swap you with someone named Amelia."

"The *day shift*?" Kallie groaned. "I can't pay my bills on the day shift!"

"She feels really guilty, like it's her fault," Mike added.

"But she already told me I can park close to the door. I don't need—"

"That detective is coming by at six o'clock, Kallie," her dad interjected. "Go on and get your rental car, so you're back before he gets here. Tess can stay, and we'll all play Trivial Pursuit when you get back."

"Dad—"

"I'm in, Mister B!" Tess answered with a laugh. "You have the night off anyway, Kal. Let's get a pizza and hang out here."

Sherman heard the word "pizza" and stuck his fuzzy head out of the bedroom door.

"See, Sherm's with us, too."

Still grumbling about having to work the day shift, Kallie agreed and left with Mike to get her rental car.

Chapter Four

"I don't want to hear one word about it," Kallie grumbled as she stalked back into the house an hour later.

"I actually like it," Mike said with a smile.

"You *would*."

"*Hey!*"

"I can't believe I'm stuck with this atrocity," Kallie complained, a little louder than she intended.

"It's not really an atroc—"

"What? *What?!*" Tess called, noticing Kallie's tone and looking up from the jigsaw puzzle that Kallie's father had started.

"Go look." Mike pointed with a laugh.

Tess walked to the window, asking, "At what? What's the big— oh." A huge, neon yellow muscle car sat in the driveway. It had bulges on ripples on curves and looked like it would sound like a motor boat. "Wow."

"It was the only car they had because of the Spring Break crowd," Kallie whined. "Someone had just returned it, or they wouldn't have had any cars available at all."

"Wasn't it expensive?" Tess asked, still staring.

"I reserved an economy car on their website, so they gave it to me for the same price."

"It's actually sort of—"

"*Awful?*"

"I was going to say cheerful. Yellow is cheerful."

"It looks like Pac-Man on steroids, Tess."

Her friend snorted to stifle her laugh. "At least it'll be easy to find at the beach."

"If you think I'm driving that hideous thing to the beach—"

Her father came back into the house from his hobby shop in the garage. "What happened? Did you get your car?" He continued straight to the window to check. "Oh! Hey, they made cars like that when you were a kid, Kallie. Not in that color, as I recall," he added, crinkling his nose at the neon. "Can I take it for a spin?"

"*Seriously?*"

"I'll go with you, Mister B!" Tess cheered, pulling Mike along and snatching the keys from Kallie's hand.

"Are you all *twelve*?!" Kallie grumped, but they were already outside and climbing into the Ugly Mobile. She had to laugh as they pulled out of the driveway, though. All of her favorite weirdos in their new clown car.

She went ahead and ordered two pizzas, since delivery would take an hour on Sunday night, and chopped up a huge romaine salad with red peppers and tomatoes. Still annoyed at the ugly car, she was much more relieved that her dear friends and family had taken her mind off the stress of the day for a while. Kallie had been worried about how she'd feel after Tess left for the evening, but now she had all of them here, making her laugh. *And this morning, I wasn't sure if I'd ever laugh again.*

Mike and Tess would probably want beer with their pizza, so she brought in a few from the garage refrigerator. By the time she'd finished and settled down to the jigsaw puzzle, her crazy crew was pulling back into the driveway in the rental Banana Barge, and she was in a better mood.

* * * * *

Kallie was chewing on a pizza crust and considering a trivia question about nineteenth-century vice presidents when she heard a car door slam. Immediately looking at the clock, she noted, "That's the detective."

"Adlai Stevenson!" she yelled her answer to the others, running to open the door just as the doorbell rang. "Hi, Detective Morrison. Come in."

"Is that your rental car, Miss Brooks? Did they not have anything in orange with purple polka dots?"

"*See?!*" she yelled at Tess, who was giggling uncontrollably. "That was the only thing they had available."

"At least you won't have trouble finding it in crowded parking lots," the detective added, a little more gently.

Kallie rolled her eyes and led the detective back to the dinner table. "My father said you had some more questions for me?"

"Yes, just a few. The way the cameras are set up in the bar, you're visible on camera virtually the entire night. It's rare that someone has a perfect alibi, but even your breaks are mostly on camera. I wanted to ask you about a few of your colleagues."

"Oh, okay. They're all really nice, but I'm guessing that's not what you want to know."

"The other bartender, Charlie, is also on camera enough to clear him, since he was behind the beachside bar all night. And Marcy was mostly in her office, which is on the same camera as the back door, so she couldn't have exited to the parking lot that way." Kallie nodded, listening. "But the employees who spend a lot of time walking around—" He read a list from his notebook, "Mike, Carlos, Melanie, Cindy, Jessi, and Tony. What can you tell me about them?"

Kallie was surprised at the question. *I've been worried about some mysterious, crazed madman stalking Owhiro, and he's asking about my friends?* "You don't really think the killer's someone who works at the bar, do you?"

"We just don't have enough information to clear them yet. Let's start with—"

"We were watching the news, and they didn't identify the girl," Kallie interrupted, changing the subject. She hoped to get a few answers out of him and knew this was her only chance. "Didn't you say it was someone local? I read that she might be a homeless person—" She glanced over at Tess, to make sure she was listening.

"That's how it appeared last night," he replied slowly, measuring his words carefully. "But her fingerprints weren't in the system, so that seems unlikely now."

"So you don't even know her name yet?"

"I really can't tell you very much at this point. We don't know much yet, but even if we did, I can't discuss an open case." Surely he faced these questions every day, and just recited his memorized deflections automatically, but he still seemed apologetic. "We'll probably have a press conference in the morning, though."

Across the table, Tess tapped a reminder into her phone and nodded at Kallie. They'd definitely be watching that Monday morning press conference together.

"Now can you tell me about Mike Jacobson, please?"

Kallie knew she was out of distractions. "You actually just missed him. He had to leave for work."

"I spoke to him last night. Right now, I'm really more interested in hearing what *you* have to say about him. All of them, actually."

"Oh. Well, Mike and I have known each other for years. We've both been working at the Lazy Gecko for about the same amount of time, and we've been friends pretty much since we first met. He's a sweetheart. There's no way he's a murderer."

"Any romantic relationship?"

"With Mike? No way, he's more like a big brother. And I'm not his type, anyway. He dates beautiful blondes with fancy cars," Kallie replied, shaking her head. "Although, technically, I have the *car* now."

The detective chuckled without looking up from his notebook.

"There's a camera on the door, right?" Kallie asked. "So wouldn't you have seen him if he went out to the parking lot?" she asked.

"He went out the beachside door, from the back bar, and was out of camera range for a while."

"Oh. Well, Mike's not a murderer, I'll tell you that much. Not a chance." She said it like the case was officially closed on that pronouncement, but she could see that the detective didn't take it that way. She squinted at his notebook in annoyance, wishing she could change his mind. *Whoever this psycho is, it's definitely not Mike.*

"We'll worry about clearing him as soon as possible, Miss Brooks. I'd just like to hear what you know about him."

"Okay, let's see… His family's from Texas. Near San Antonio, I think. But he's lived in Florida for at least six years, and he has a condo here in Owhiro. He's very protective of me and Melanie. I don't know Cindy and Jessi very well, since they don't work in my section, but I've seen him looking out for other female customers, too."

"Can you think of any reason for him to go out of the beachside door at midnight?"

"Sure, of course. I mean, that's his job, right? He makes sure everything's safe and nothing creepy happens outside, and no one gets hurt. He might've seen some drunk college girl stumbling out in the dark, or someone starting a fight—"

Kallie paused, thinking of the poor girl who'd lost her fight. *And begged for my help in that dream… where I couldn't help her either.*

Detective Morrison gave her a moment, and

then flipped the page in his notebook. "This is very helpful, Miss Brooks. Can we move on to Carlos Alvarez now?"

Kallie had to smile. "Carlos is the sweetest guy. He looks like a muscle-head, and all the girls are crazy over him. But he's a homebody with a beautiful pregnant wife, and he's so excited to be a girl dad. Did you see him outside of the camera range too?"

"Only for a few minutes."

"So you're mostly worried about Mike? Mike is the nicest—"

"Please try not to worry about who we're investigating, Miss Brooks." He set the notebook down and looked at her seriously. "You've had a tough day, and I don't want to make it any worse. Let *us* do the worrying, ok? We need to check out everyone, so we can clear them. It's not personal."

Kallie nodded, trying to believe him.

"You've already said you don't know much about Jessi or Cindy, so let's talk about Tony."

Kallie laughed. "Tony isn't your guy. I don't work closely with him, and the girls all love him, but he'd lose his head if it wasn't stapled on. He's dumber than a bag of oatmeal."

The detective snorted a laugh but added in a serious tone, "Understood. And Melanie?"

"Have you met Melanie? She's a hundred

pounds soaking wet. No way she could move a body."

"But her personality? Is she the angry type?"

"Oh, not at all. She's a bubbly sweetheart with a boyfriend who adores her." Kallie leaned forward on her elbows over the dinner table. "Marcy doesn't tolerate nasty people, Detective. She might have to sell them drinks, but she wouldn't put up with a mean or aggressive employee for ten seconds."

Detective Morrison looked up from his notes and made eye contact with Kallie, understanding her point. He nodded sincerely.

"Thank you, Miss Brooks. This is all very helpful." He closed his notebook and stood up. "Try not to worry about Mike Jacobson. We need to check him out, but if he's innocent, this will all shake out in the next few days."

Chapter Five

"Hi, Kallie. Is your father home?" a cloyingly sweet voice called from the sidewalk as Kallie came back with the newspaper the next morning.

"Oh, hello, Mrs. Carter," Kallie replied, groaning to herself inwardly. "No, I'm sorry, he's not—"

But it was too late. Like a panther on the prowl, her father's latest huntress had elbowed her way straight into the living room.

"Yoo hoo, Benny," she called loudly. "I brought your favorite German chocolate cake." In her mind, Kallie could picture her father crouched behind the scroll saw in the garage, hiding for his life. The elderly widows in the neighborhood all had his number and stalked him like he was a badly injured, mature but still handsome gazelle. Kallie rolled her eyes.

"I'm sorry, Mrs. Carter. I'll let him know you stopped by." She accepted the cake as payment for the annoying intrusion, setting it on the table, then tried taking the woman's arm to lead her back to the door, but she was roughly shaken off. The woman's spidery mascara and brilliant fuchsia lipstick belied the strength and impatience of a Buccaneers linebacker.

"Where is he?" she growled, not one to be dismissed. "I saw his car in the backyard."

"You looked in the backyard? Did you climb the fence?" Kallie asked, unsure whether to be amused or alarmed. She briefly wondered if the detective might still be in the neighborhood, and then she remembered that this was actually *her* house.

Swiping the elderly woman by the shoulder and tucking a hand into her lower back, she manhandled her a few steps toward the door before the intruder gave up and started walking willingly. "I need to do laundry now, Mrs. Carter, so you'll need to go home. I'll tell my father that you stopped by." Depositing her on the front porch, she closed the door quickly and waved goodbye through the window. After a moment's thought, she locked the deadbolt.

Kallie walked back toward the kitchen, grumbling to herself, and noticed as the pantry door slowly creaked open and crinkly blue eyes peeked out.

"Is she gone?"

"She's gone."

"What a strange woman," Kallie's father commented, sounding a bit confused.

"Well she thinks you're a catch, Dad," Kallie explained with a laugh.

"I don't know about all that, but I don't think I need catching. And she seems a little— Oooh, German chocolate cake!"

* * * * *

Kallie and Tess met for breakfast as planned and waited for the press conference, which was scheduled to start at nine a.m. The live broadcast finally broke into the local news at 9:35 a.m.

The Owhiro police station didn't have many officers, being such a small town, so the mayor handled the introductions. Only three of the local television stations had arrived with cameras, and she addressed them directly.

"I'm the mayor of Owhiro, Rebecca Torres," she began. "This press conference has been called to discuss the murder on Saturday night." She sounded awkward and a bit nervous, and Kallie realized this was probably her first murder case. "I'm going to hand the discussion over to the Owhiro police chief, Cab Patterson."

The police chief, whom Kallie had met a few times at the Lazy Gecko during charity events, entered the screen and took his place at the podium. He seemed much more comfortable. "On Saturday night, the body of a young woman was found outside a popular night club in Owhiro—"

"It's not really a night club," Kallie grumbled, her forkful of breakfast burrito held in midair.

43

"The circumstances were unusual, and at this time we believe she was the victim of foul play. It seems as if her clothing and appearance were changed to delay her identification," the chief continued. "As of yet, we've been unable to identify her, and there have been no missing person reports matching her description, so we're asking for the public's help. The victim has shoulder-length blonde hair and unusual blue-green eyes. She was about five foot two inches tall and just over one hundred pounds, and we believe she was in her early twenties. Unfortunately, she has no identifying markings – no tattoos or even birthmarks – and was wearing no jewelry."

There was some chatter from the reporters as they absorbed that.

"I know this is vague, and we'll try to get a sketch out to the media soon, but it's very important that the public contact us right away if you've noticed your friend or family member missing and she matches this description. Please call 9-1-1 or the local anonymous tip line if you have any information."

The local crime tip line phone number appeared at the bottom of Kallie's television screen as the police chief gestured to the reporters for questions.

"The original report said that she might have been homeless?" a reporter asked.

"The way she was dressed made it seem like she may have fallen on hard times. But the coroner now thinks she was re-dressed after her murder."

"Isn't it unusual for someone to be missing this long without being reported?" another voice called out.

"It is a little odd, but missing persons are often reported by their employers when they miss work. Since it happened over the weekend, we're hoping for break today as people return to work."

A few more questions were shouted, but the chief indicated that he had to leave and turned the podium back over to the mayor. "Thank you for coming, and we'll schedule another press conf—"

"That wasn't very helpful," Kallie whispered to Tess, while still listening.

"Yeah, it doesn't sound like they really know anything yet," Tess agreed, poking a chunk of potato with her fork as the news channel cut back to the anchor desk.

* * * * *

After the press conference, Tess had to leave for work, and Marcy called to insist that Kallie take another day off.

As she hugged Tess goodbye and promised to meet her after work, Kallie's stomach did somersaults at the thought of being left alone all day.

Tess worked as a receptionist for an elderly

lawyer in Owhiro, with the extraordinary name of Cornelius Nicodemus Winchester, Esquire, who had been a prominent legal fixture in the Tampa Bay area thirty years earlier. He had very little interest in practicing law anymore, but even less interest in moldering away in his otherwise empty mansion.

Tess wasn't a paralegal and didn't even have a degree in law – she had been a Business Administration major, but Winchester liked her moxie. Tess was a small, curvy brunette with long eyelashes and a wickedly sharp sense of humor. She was also a bona fide, certified genius, which she confessed to almost no one. Most guys thought she was sexy until they ran afoul of her brilliant mind and caustic wit – and then they either ran for the hills or became puppy-dog obsessed.

Winchester was the outlier. That wit made her the perfect receptionist for his strategy – she'd scare off the boring, run-of-the-mill legal requests, but she was smart enough to catch the ones that might yet interest him. He wasn't retired, after all.

She sometimes complained that the job was boring, but Kallie knew she liked the research opportunities, and she'd grown quite attached to the venerable old attorney.

It was already hot outside, even though it wasn't even eleven a.m., and Kallie poured a tall glass of her favorite ice-cold lemonade and carried a book outside

46

to the patio. *If I'm forced to take the day off without pay, I might as well try to enjoy it,* she told herself.

It only took a few minutes of reading quietly before her mind started to wander, though. Every branch waving in the faint breeze looked like the sign of a stalker in the bushes. Each duck's awkward flight past her seat made her jump in shock. She went back inside to get Sherman, who didn't usually care for the heat of midday, hoping his presence would calm her down.

"There's nothing to be worried about, right, Sherm?" she asked him softly, scratching his ears. She'd brought out a bowl of ice water for him, and he rested his head on her knee protectively between drinks.

Even he became jumpy, though – probably feeding off her nerves. He usually liked to watch the herons and anhingas relaxing by the water, and the occasional paddleboarder on the lake, but he was watching everything too closely. When he barked at a squirrel on the lower deck, Kallie gave up on the idea, and they both went back inside.

"Fine, then," she told Sherman, "I'll wash my hair, since I did a terrible job of it yesterday."

Sherman didn't complain, of course, so Kallie turned up the air conditioning a little and ran a hot bath. Rummaging through the bathroom closet for bubble bath, which wasn't usually her style, she settled on a fizzing bath bomb that smelled like lilacs.

Kallie clearly remembered locking the front

door after Tess left and bolting the back door after she came back inside from the patio, but she couldn't resist checking them both anyway.

When she finally settled into the fizzy, sweet-smelling bathtub and tuned into the '80s station on her in-shower radio, she felt better than she'd felt in days. She didn't notice how tense her muscles had become until they hit the hot water and started to relax.

Sherman opened the lever handle of the bathroom door with his paw, a trick he'd taught himself, and walked over to sniff the water. Kallie scratched his ears, reminded of just how smart he really was – a famous trait of his primary breed – and pushed the door shut again.

"Bored already, huh?"

Sherman laid down on the cool tiled bathroom floor and immediately went back to napping.

Kallie leaned back on the sloped bathtub wall and started to doze off herself, when a voice in her head whispered, *He'll find you, too.*

It was the voice from her dream, the faceless, dead blonde girl. *He found me, and now he'll find you. Why did you talk to the police?*

Kallie didn't think for an instant that it was some ghostly communication from the dead. This was the start of a panic attack, and she needed to control it, *now*. As she sat still and tried to take deep breaths to calm down, the fear boiled up in her mind, and then deep within her chest.

He's going to find you.

He's going to kill you.

You'll end up like me...

Jumping out of the bathtub and grabbing a towel, startling Sherman awake, Kallie threw her dirty clothes back on with shaking hands and dashed out of the room. She didn't even pause before reaching the front door, grabbing Sherman's leash and water bottle, and running down the front steps with him to escape.

* * * * *

Kallie's mother called again that night, forcing her mind back to her brother. She wasn't very close to either of them, but she was happy for the distraction. Her mother had always been self-centered and shallow, thinking more about money and herself than her family. Her brother was the same, except he also had addiction issues. Kallie couldn't imagine how they were related to her, and even less to her father, but she loved them anyway. Mostly. *Family ties outweigh constant vexation.*

"Hello, Mother," Kallie answered the phone. She hated being called *mom*, which drove Kallie crazy.

"Hello Kalliope Lynn," she replied. Kallie gritted her teeth at being called by her full name, and she reminded herself about family outweighing vexation again.

"Sorry I didn't call you back this morning. We've had some excitement around here. You probably saw it on the news."

"You know I don't watch the news, dear." Without bothering to ask about Kallie's situation, she immediately jumped into her concern about Jack, Kallie's brother. The golden child, despite his many issues. "Jack still hasn't returned my calls or texted me back. Have you heard from him?"

"You know Jack doesn't talk to me, Mother."

"Well, you could try calling him to see if he's okay."

"If he's not answering your calls, why on earth would he answer me?" *You're the one with the money, Mother*, she thought to herself. *That's all he cares about, and he knows I don't have a dime.*

She considered for a brief moment that her brother might have had a run-in with the Lazy Gecko murderer, looking for revenge on Kallie, but shook it off. *Jack has more than enough problems, and enemies, without creating a conspiracy.*

"Is your father there?" She was jerked back into the conversation.

Kallie's dad was reading a spy novel on the couch, but Kallie wasn't giving him up. "Sorry, Mother.

He's stepped out for a walk." Her dad raised a hand in silent thanks, without looking up from his book. Even if her mother hadn't just divorced her fourth husband, Kallie considered her dad officially off-limits. "Jack wouldn't talk to him either, if that's what you're thinking."

Her mother snorted in annoyance.

"Have you tried calling the police, Mother?" Kallie sighed into the phone.

"Kalliope! Don't say such things!" her mother gasped theatrically.

"Please. He posts bail around here so often, they have Mercedes police cars. They know him so well, the cops invite him to Thanksgiving dinner."

"That's not funny!"

On the contrary, her father snorted into his book.

"Look, I'll tell him you're looking for him, if for some reason he contacts me. Did you need anything else?"

"Can't a mother just—"

"Great talking to you, Mom. Bye."

She hung up as her mother yelled "*Don't call me M—*" into the receiver.

With her serenity wrecked for the evening, Kallie turned to her dad. "Want to go for an actual walk around the lake?"

"Sure do, kiddo. Let me just get my shoes."

* * * * *

Kallie's quaint old neighborhood in Owhiro had been built around a large natural lake, and they often took Sherman out for walks on the circular path around it, where he could bark at the ducks and visit his other doggie friends. Tonight, after he'd had a chance to greet Ripley the corgi and Charlie the chocolate lab, Kallie and her dad had a chance to talk.

"They still haven't identified the girl, huh?" her dad asked, gently.

Kallie's heart raced a little, but she couldn't shut it out any longer. She needed to talk about the murder, and the victim, before her lurking fears grew worse. "She didn't have any ID or a phone, and her fingerprints didn't come up in the police system either."

"So she'd never been arrested. Not even for petty theft or trespassing," Kallie's father mused. "And she probably doesn't work for a hospital or a school."

"Oh, I didn't think of that."

"And they fingerprint you for a concealed weapon license too, so she mustn't have that either. Or maybe she's just not from Florida," he shrugged.

"The police asked for help from the public during the press conference, but she didn't have any tattoos or even a birthmark, so there won't be much help with identification until someone reports her missing."

"Well, hopefully she has a nine-to-five job. If so, then she missed work today, obviously. A lot of people work remotely, but surely her boss would've noticed that she was absent. And tomorrow, too."

"Maybe."

Sherman sniffed a small turtle beside the path, and then decided it was a new toy, picking it up proudly and showing it to his family. "Sherman, drop it!" Kallie snapped.

Disappointed, her dog plunked the now-closed turtle back in the grass, and Kallie carried it closer to the trees, where it would be safer.

"Even with the way everyone is so isolated these days, you'd think someone would have noticed a young lady missing."

"Well, you know Tess and her online investigations. She said the local crime bloggers that she follows are having a field day with their research now," Kallie reassured him. "Missing persons reports and photos are arriving from all over the country for comparison. It shouldn't be too much longer before someone figures it out."

Chapter Six

After a few days passed without anyone reporting the missing young woman, Kallie was beginning to wonder if she would ever be identified. Then on Wednesday morning, the police finally caught a break.

The morning anchor on the Tampa Bay 24-hour news station had mentioned a new lead in the case, but she didn't have any details – so naturally, Tess showed up at nine a.m. with bagels. Kallie and Tess found themselves parked on the couch again, this time with Kallie's dad equally fascinated, waiting for the latest press conference to start.

"It *must* be big news," her dad noted, pointing at the screen when the live feed started. "They aren't starting with Mayor Torres this time."

The Pinellas County Sheriff's media relations officer took the podium this time – a sharp woman in a beautifully tailored suit, who seemed to have been raised in front of a camera. There was a lot of precursory discussion with the press, and the liaison spelled several officers' names out loud, including her own. Then she introduced the Owhiro chief of police.

"There has still been no response from the public, and no one has come forward to personally identify the Owhiro murder victim. However, the St Pete medical examiner has received a match on her out-of-state dental records," Chief Patterson told the viewing public. A young officer approached the podium and placed a large rectangular board on nearby easel, which the chief unveiled theatrically, showing a pretty young blonde with interesting, pale eyes and an easy smile. "Her name is Alexandra Clemons, age twenty-four, from Sarasota."

There was a murmur of interest from the reporters as they finally saw the face of the previous weekend's murder victim. She wasn't strikingly beautiful, but her face was pretty and peaceful, and there was an instant likeability to her expression. She was someone you wanted to know, and never would. Tess took Kallie's hand, as they both teared up at the sight.

"Alexandra moved to Florida recently, with plans to start her own business," the chief of police continued. "We don't have a lot more information on her final days yet, but we're hoping the local community can help us. Please remember that this young woman was murdered in our own hometown. If you saw something, please say something." He closed his eyes and took a breath before continuing.

"Alexandra's father has flown down from his home in Washington, DC, and he's going to address the media. Mr. Clemons?"

The chief stepped away from the podium and a tall, greying man in a rumpled suit walked into the television screen. He introduced himself as Robert Clemons, but he didn't spell it. His voice was even, but the dark circles under his reddened eyes told another story. Kallie couldn't imagine the heartbreak he was enduring.

"Alexandra was my only daughter, my only child," he explained. "Nothing can bring her back, so I can only ask you all for... closure – whatever that is." He paused, miserably. Looking straight into the camera, he concluded, "Please, I'm begging all of you, if you know anything about her death, please call the police. Call the tip line. I'm personally offering a reward, in addition to the tip line reward. So please—" His voice cracked, and he stopped, turning away.

He had only spoken for thirty seconds, but Kallie was shaken to the core by his emptiness. She leaned on her dad's shoulder and watched as the media relations officer returned to the podium. She picked up the oversized photograph and carried it back to where the news cameras could get a good angle, seemingly a little cold, but effectively doing her very difficult job. She gave the tip line number again and emphasized that any tip could help, even the tiniest detail that might seem inconsequential.

"If you saw *anything* unusual at or around the

Lazy Gecko on Saturday night, please give us a call," she stoically implored. "Anything. Don't worry if it seems silly or useless. Let us do the research and figure that out." She mentioned the reward again, and the station cut back to the regular news cycle.

* * * * *

Kallie was starting her new job on the day shift at the Lazy Gecko in just over an hour and didn't want to be late, but she and Tess couldn't resist checking the online news on her laptop before she left. The crime bloggers had somehow already discovered Alexandra's father and researched his whole life. *Helpful but creepy*, Kallie thought to herself.

The Clemons family was spectacularly rich with manufacturing money, the shrewd bloggers had discovered, and Alexandra's mother had passed away from ovarian cancer just two years earlier. Alexandra, or Lex as she was known, was an only child who had moved to Florida after college to start a charity working with foster kids. Now her father was left with no one.

So why did Morrison think she was homeless, if she was super rich? Kallie wondered. *Why did no one notice that such a high-profile young lady was missing? And what was she doing at a tiny bar in Owhiro after midnight, over an hour from her home in Sarasota?* Lex was apparently no longer a Spring Break partier, although she was the same age as many of them. She was already running an important charity and helping kids — it didn't mesh with that unruly crowd. *One last wild party, maybe?*

The "Owhiro Murder" story, as it was being called, had already become national news, but mostly in spotlight pieces because of the weird circumstances of the crime scene. Now it was blowing up like a runaway hot air balloon. The only daughter of a famous, wealthy family, murdered in an inconspicuous little beach town? It would be on every television screen, phone, and computer monitor in America by noon.

As much as Kallie would've liked to forget the whole ordeal and get on with her life, she felt herself getting *more* attached to the murder. It wasn't just because she was close to it, physically, by way of her job and her car. She felt a growing connection to Alexandra Clemons. Maybe it was just the haunting nightmares where Lex called out to her, begging for help, but she felt a strange obligation stirring in her heart.

Against her better judgment, and cursing her own madness, she decided to see if she could help.

Some of the crime blogs that Tess followed had picked up and posted the Owhiro Murder story right away, within eight hours, and some even displayed their own photos – so Kallie knew they must be nearby. After work, since she'd have some time in the evening with her new daytime schedule, she promised herself she'd try to contact a few of them. Detective Morrison had already stalled on telling her anything else about the murder, but she thought she could wrangle some information out of the local, connected bloggers once they knew the role she played in the case.

I'm not going to play the 'Don't you know who I am?!' card, she told herself — and then decided that, if necessary, she just might.

* * * * *

"Hey, Marcy." Kallie stood in the office doorway, awkward and unfamiliar with the bar in daylight.

Marcy sent her office chair spinning away into the wall as she jumped up and ran to hug Kallie. "Oh my gosh, I didn't sleep at all this week, girl. How are you?"

Kallie hugged her back warmly. "I'm fine. I'm not sleeping well either, but right now I'm more worried about working this weird shift. I've been a night person for so long."

After working at the Lazy Gecko for six years, it was almost like a second home to Kallie, but she was always there on the night shift. Her internal clock was completely bamboozled.

"I'm hoping it won't be for too long," Marcy tried to reassure her. "I want to wait until this killer gets

59

caught, so I'm not worried about him coming back to—
"

"Bump me off?" Kallie asked with a grin.

"I was going to say 'clean up loose ends,' but yeah. Bump you off."

"I can't say it hasn't occurred to me, honestly. But I obviously didn't see anything, since I was working all night."

"I'm not sure a crazed psycho killer will be thinking that logically, Kal. Sorry to burst your bubble."

Kallie's stomach started tightening up in knots again, and she changed the subject quickly. "Can we talk about these daytime hours, instead? I can't afford a cut in my tips, Marcy."

"I don't think you'll have a problem. The lunch crowd varies a little from day to day, but the afternoon and happy hour crowds are full of regulars, and most of them tip well. You'll probably make more on weekdays and less on Saturdays, so it should even out."

Kallie had worked in places where bartenders worked from open to close, which could be a twelve-plus hour day. But the Lazy Gecko had a day shift and a night shift — she would be setting up at ten a.m., doors open at eleven a.m., and leaving at seven p.m. It seemed like a completely different universe from leaving at three a.m. The nighttime world was familiar and comfortable to her — she knew all of the stores and pizza places that were open in the middle of the night.

And they all knew her.

"I know you're not used to doing the morning setup before we open, so I'll show you around and then you can talk to Amelia," Marcy explained, walking Kallie toward the door. "She'll be switching shifts with you for now, but I asked her to come in today and show you the ropes."

They walked out of the office and back into the bar. "Have they given your car back yet?"

"No," Kallie grumbled. "It's still being checked for evidence. I have a rental car."

"Oh, that's nice.

"You're only saying that because you haven't seen it," Kallie replied with a grimace. "I'll show you later."

"Do you think you'll keep your car? After they return it?"

"What do you mean?"

"I mean, after the... after all that's happened."

"Oh. I hadn't thought about it, actually." Kallie stood still and thought for a moment about the nightmare in her back seat. "No, probably not. I guess I should start saving up for a new car, too." *Like I need one more expense, and another thing to worry about right now,* she thought to herself. "You're pretty sure my tips will be okay on this shift?"

"Why don't you talk to Amelia about that too?"

* * * * *

After "the incident," as everyone at the Lazy Gecko had started calling it, the subject of the parking lot's safety kept creeping up. Kallie wasn't really worried, even working after dark, as long as she could park in the well-lit spaces near the door. She trusted Carlos and Mike completely, and she tried telling Marcy that, but her friend and boss wasn't having any of it.

"You're parking in the spot right next to the door, and you're working during daylight hours," she insisted. "I don't know what I was thinking having you park all the way back by the street. The guys can park back there, but your little car isn't taking up any extra space." She still hadn't forgiven herself, and was convinced that she had personally put Kallie's life in danger.

"Marcy, there was no way of knowing—"

"It could have been you."

"But it *wasn't!*"

No matter how much anxiety Kallie had felt in the past few days, she never for an instant blamed Marcy. She didn't know who the murderer was yet, but *he* was the one to blame. *Now I just need to convince Marcy of that.*

And so the argument went around and around,

while Kallie put up with the coddling and the weird hours – and worried about the tips.

She quickly found that there was a completely dissimilar type of clientele during the day. There were still a few college kids, the last of the Spring Breakers, but the day-drinking locals were a different breed. Some were retirees, and some were just rich folks with nothing better to do. A few seemed to be meeting not-very-secret romantic partners. At least they were all interesting.

The Lazy Gecko was a quirky, charming bar in a nice neighborhood with a beautiful view of the beach, but Kallie had never really known why the place was so unusually popular. They always had five-star reviews in the travel magazines, regardless of the fact that they were in a small town and off the normal tourist track.

She quickly discovered, to her surprise, that the bar had a spectacular kitchen. She rarely sold food at night, other than the standard bar fare of nachos and buffalo wings, so she was stunned to see the crowd picking up at lunch. *Surely all of these people aren't getting drunk on their lunch hour,* she wondered as the booths started filling up before noon.

Apparently the Lazy Gecko was the best lunch spot in town. People drove to Owhiro from their offices in Clearwater and Palm Harbor for the distinctive menu. Even the salad and sandwich combo left patrons raving.

"Bring me a Bloody Mary, could you please?" a middle-aged man with grey hair and a friendly smile called to her as he took a seat at the bar. "No celery. And a bowl of that amazing seafood chowder."

"We have seafood chowder?" Kallie mumbled to herself, grabbing a menu.

"It's the special on Wednesdays," he told her, leaving her feeling like an outsider in her own bar. "I come in every Wednesday just for a bowl."

"That good?"

"You should try it," he added with a laugh. "Before it sells out."

"Uh. I'll do that."

"With the sourdough bread."

"*Seriously?*" She flipped the menu over, looking at the back, and then tried to find a menu board for the specials.

"Are you new?"

"What? Oh, no. Sorry, I usually work the night shift."

He introduced himself as Teddy McNally and pointed out a few other lunchtime regulars after Kallie had placed his kitchen order for the soup.

"Let me get you that Bloody Mary." She poured Teddy the tall, hearty drink, adding pickled asparagus in place of the celery, and a pair of bacon corkscrews – plus extra hot sauce by request.

"Now that's the prettiest drink I think I've ever seen," he proclaimed happily. "Too bad it's already too hot to sit outside — this has been a brutal spring. This would be a perfect drink for sitting out on the patio."

He was right, and the Lazy Gecko had a beautiful little outdoor patio overlooking the beach, but April was always one of the hottest months of the year. It rarely rained in central Florida in the spring, but this year had brought an even worse drought than normal.

"Luckily, the view from the windows is almost as pretty."

Chapter Seven

The next morning, Tess and Kallie were watching the police press conference, as always. The Pinellas County Sheriff's media relations officer introduced herself again, and she explained who would be speaking. Then the chief of police stepped up to the microphone to continue.

"Good morning," he welcomed the press and the viewers. "We want to share some more information with you on the Owhiro nightclub murder this morning." Alexandra's photo was resting on an easel next to him, as usual.

"The fiancé of Alexandra Clemons, who had previously been reported as a person of interest in the case, has been located, and he's cooperating with police. He has asked to make a public statement, and while that's not common practice, we're going to allow it due to his assistance. He'll be speaking to the press after we're finished with the new details."

"Do you have a cause of death?" one of the reporters called out, although the chief hadn't yet asked for questions.

The chief frowned in annoyance at the

interruption but gestured offscreen, and another man approached the podium. "This is the Pinellas County medical examiner, Doctor David Patel."

The chief stepped aside as the doctor spelled his name for the press, which Kallie always found vaguely amusing, and quickly got to the point. "The autopsy was finished last night, and the results show conclusively that Miss Clemons was killed by blunt force trauma to the head," he announced. "There were additional injuries after the fact, involved with her placement into the vehicle. DNA and toxicology results have not been returned yet, and my team will update you when they are received. I won't be taking any questions from the media at this time."

The doctor walked casually out of the camera view without even a backward glance at the dumbstruck reporters. The police chief returned to the podium awkwardly, looking a little stunned, like he wished he could smoothly refuse all questions too.

"The victim, Alexandra Clemons," he resumed, "lived in a small one-bedroom, one-bath rental house, owned by an antiques dealer in Sarasota. She also worked in the area. The local and county police have searched the victim's home and office, and spoken with her landlord. The landlord was cooperating with police but has since disappeared. We're looking for him now, as well as two other individuals who may have seen something. We'll distribute photos to you all before we leave," he addressed the reporters.

"We've heard that Alexandra's family is very wealthy" an older, reputable male reporter from a national cable news channel called out. "Is there any indication that this was related to her family's money? A disgruntled employee? Or a kidnapping situation that went bad?"

Kallie had, of course, read about the family's fortune online, but it hadn't been publicized widely on the local news. This was an angle she really hadn't considered. *Would someone travel all this way, and commit murder, just to hurt the victim's father? Maybe.*

"We don't believe this event is related to her father or the money at this time. The details seem to point in a different direction, but we haven't eliminated any motives or suspects yet. The investigation is very fluid."

"Do you have any information on the landlord's disappearance? The antiques dealer? Do you believe he's in any danger?" a female reporter asked.

"We stopped at both his home and the antique shop, but it appears he's left town. The owner of the restaurant next door to his shop notified us that he packed up his truck yesterday and said he was going to visit friends in Alabama. Or Arkansas. She couldn't remember which. She said it didn't seem strange at the time, because he goes on shopping trips to other states all the time. It's part of his job. But, of course, when the police show up, everything looks nefarious."

"Was it illegal for him to leave town?"

"No, it was inconvenient, but not illegal," the chief clarified. "He won't be arrested; we would just like to find him for some further questioning."

"Had the restaurant owner ever seen Miss Clemons visiting the landlord at his shop?" another reporter called out.

"She wasn't sure. It's a fairly popular shopping area with a lot of foot traffic. We're waiting for surveillance video from the restaurant's security company, which may be some help. We also don't know how well Alexandra actually knew her landlord. Most of the rental transaction – like many these days – was done online before she moved to Florida."

The police chief abruptly interrupted the media questions to introduce Alexandra's fiancé, James Davis, who came to the podium looking annoyed and grumpy, like he was being rudely kept from an appointment.

"Good morning," he addressed the media. "I'm James Davis, and I was planning to marry Alexandra Clemons in the fall." His eyes were dry, voice calm, and his attitude seemed more disgruntled than heartbroken.

"As you all know, there are multiple rewards for information regarding her murder. I think it's something like fifty thousand dollars now, combined. The cops told us that there was probably at least one accomplice needed, which means there's a witness out there somewhere." He casually waved his hand at the cameras to symbolize the sea of viewers. "That's a big wad of cash for someone, and all you need to do is leave an anonymous message on the tip line."

Kallie's lip curled reflexively at this man's callous discussion of money while talking about the murder of his fiancée.

"That kind of money could change your life, and you'd be helping Robert Clemons and the cops." He looked offscreen at someone, nodded, and then walked away from the podium without another word.

"Gee, he seemed really broken up, didn't he?" Tess asked, voice dripping with sarcasm, echoing Kallie's thoughts.

After watching Alexandra's father and his broken heart, the fiancé seemed like an emotionless robot with nothing on his mind but the cash.

"Did he even mention Lex at all?" *What a slimy jerk.*

Kallie reminded herself that everyone processes grief differently, but she instantly disliked and distrusted the fiancé. When he stopped talking, the station immediately cut back to their regular news, almost as if they felt the same sense of disgust at his crass manner.

"An antiques dealer?" Tess noted, thinking back on the police chief's statement. "That doesn't seem like the kind of job that would pay for an investment property."

Kallie answered, "Depends on how long he's been in the area. If he bought the place cheap ten years ago, he could make a killing on rent now."

"No pun intended?"

* * * * *

"Can I get you anything?" Kallie asked the last lunch guest remaining by mid-afternoon. She didn't usually stray from behind the bar at night, but it was the slow period between lunch and happy hour. The guy had been sitting in a booth for a few hours, writing unceasingly in a notebook.

"Oh, hi," he looked up, surprised to see her. "Are you new?"

"Not really," she smiled at the question, which was becoming a constant theme. "I've just always worked on the night shift."

"Sorry, I've been distracted today. I'd love another beer and an order of chicken nachos. Thanks for checking on me," he laughed. "You know I'm being absentminded when I even forget to order beer."

"No problem," Kallie smiled back. He was a studious-looking guy with wire-rimmed glasses and a neat grey goatee, but a contagious smile.

"I'd probably have starved over here. Just a skeleton propped up in the booth by five o'clock."

"Well, you won't starve with these nachos. I saw a few orders at lunch, and they're enough to feed a small army. Back in a few." She wrote down the order and walked it back to the kitchen herself – unaccustomed to the lull and glad to have something non-sinister to occupy her mind.

"Are these for Barry?" the chef asked when she handed over the order.

Kallie was surprised at the question. "He didn't say. Mid-fifties with glasses?"

"He usually orders extra jalapeños. It's not that guy?"

"Let me run back and check. I don't want to drown the wrong guy in hot peppers."

Walking quickly back out to the bar, she paused at the same booth. "Are you Barry?" she asked.

"Uh, yes?" he looked a little startled.

"The chef thought you'd like extra jalapeños, so I wanted to make sure."

"Wow, I guess that's when you know you're a regular," he joked, self-deprecatingly. "Yes, please. Extra jalapeños, and no chopped tomatoes or olives. See, I told you I was distracted."

* * * * *

"So is everything settled after the drama last weekend?" Teddy asked, now seated on his usual barstool, when Kallie came back with Barry's nachos. Teddy's wife had joined him at the bar — a lovely, wild, blonde, middle-aged bohemian lady with bright lipstick and an even brighter multi-colored flowered sundress.

"Oh, uh, drama?" Kallie asked hesitantly, scrubbing an invisible spot on the counter so she wouldn't need to make eye contact.

"Yeah, it was on the news. That girl was found dead outside this bar, right?"

Kallie continued to feign cluelessness as the knot in her stomach threatened to reappear. "Oh, *that*. Yeah, everything's *totally* back to normal. The police said it wasn't related to us. They don't think she ever even came inside the bar."

"Didn't you say you worked the night shift until recently?"

Kallie stifled a groan and switched from the invisible smudge on the bar to an invisible spot on a wine glass. *Can we please not talk about this?* she wished silently at him, but to no avail.

"I worked the night shift, but I don't know anything about the dead girl," she insisted, focusing intently on the glass.

Her nightmares had diminished a little, but she

still wasn't ready to talk about it, especially with strangers. And she didn't want anyone to think badly about the Lazy Gecko just because some psycho picked their parking lot for his grisly crime.

"Not talking, huh?" Teddy asked with a laugh. "I won't grill you for the gory details — we just like to gossip. Cecilia and I were actually here that afternoon, you know — which is unusual for us on a Saturday. So you can imagine how shocked we were to see it on the news the next morning."

"I can imagine," Kallie replied sincerely, relieved that the topic had steered away from her. *Believe me, I can imagine.*

"I even wanted to stay here a little longer that evening and watch the band, but Cici had plans with her brother," he nodded toward his wife. "Most folks our age don't like the Spring Break crowd, but they remind me of when we were young and stupid. Invincible."

"We're still invincible," Cici reminded him, toasting against his glass.

"Invincible or invisible?" he replied loudly, with a joking motion toward his ear as if he couldn't hear her. "*WHAT?!*"

His wife smacked his arm with her purse. "Insensible." She shook her head at Kallie and rolled her eyes theatrically.

Kallie loved watching the two of them goof around, even though she barely knew them. Doesn't every girl hope she'll find the one true love who still thinks she's funny and beautiful, still the brightest star in the room, when age and gravity start winning the battle?

Chapter Eight

Kallie sat at the kitchen table the next morning, still adjusting to daylight hours and googling the latest news on the murder case. Finally, Sherman walked up and put his fuzzy chin on her thigh.

When she didn't stop reading right away, he pushed down with his chin a little harder.

"I'm sorry, Sherm," she finally said, scratching his mismatched black and white floppy ears. "It stresses you out when I'm stressed out, huh?"

He just sighed.

Kallie didn't think he needed another walk, he was just worried about her. She wasn't usually a nervous person, even when bills were late and her brother was annoying and her ex was being a pest. She loved her life and her friends — and her human and canine roommates — so she was always pretty level-headed. This murder was throwing her for a loop. But she couldn't shake the sudden urge to answer Lex's nightmare pleas for help, especially after seeing her shady fiancé on the news.

"Let's go for a walk anyway, what do you say?" she asked Sherman, shaking it off for the moment.

Sherman walked to a small stool next to the front door and happily picked up his leash, carrying it back to Kallie while she tied her tennis shoes.

"That's my smart boy," she murmured, happy to be getting outside too.

* * * * *

Kallie didn't normally answer her phone while she was out walking with Sherman — often she didn't even bother to bring it along — but she checked the ID when it rang this time and saw that it was Detective Morrison. Hoping that he'd have some information for her, about her car if not the case, she answered it.

"Hello?"

"Hi, Miss Brooks. It's Detective Morrison. I'm in Owhiro for the morning on an unrelated case, and I was wondering if you could meet for a few minutes?"

"Oh, I really don't have time right now. I'm walking my dog, and I need to leave for work when we get home."

"I see. I'm not far from your house, could I meet you on your walk?"

"Oh, yeah, I suppose that would be okay," she answered, a little confused. "We're just walking around the lake."

"Great, thank you. I'll see you in a few minutes."

They both hung up and Kallie continued walking with Sherman, but her curiosity was buzzing. *What could be so important that a busy detective would drop everything for a walk? Why didn't he just tell me on the phone?* Her mind spun in a darker direction, unbidden. *What if it's bad news? Maybe Marcy was right and I'm in danger after all, and he wants to warn me in person?*

Ten minutes later, when Kallie and Sherman had walked and sniffed their way to the end of the lake, she heard a rustle behind them.

"Miss Brooks," the detective called, chuckling.

She turned and saw Detective Morrison walking quickly toward her, with his hands full of plastic bags.

"I stopped at the corner store and picked up a few things, so I don't make you too late for work." From one of the shopping bags, he pulled out a bottle of orange juice, a bag of Doritos, and a bag of sour gummy bears. He handed them over to her, keeping a bottle of water for Sherman.

"You have a good memory," Kallie replied, baffled.

"It's in the job description," Morrison answered humbly, while puncturing the lid of the water bottle with a small knife on his keychain. "But those are my *personal* favorite brand of gummy bears."

He turned the punctured water bottle over and sprayed the ice-cold contents straight into Sherman's mouth, to the dog's complete delight. "I don't have a bowl," the detective explained.

"He doesn't seem to mind," Kallie answered, with a grin at her dog's obvious amusement. "I hope he doesn't expect me to do that at home." She opened the gummy bears and ate a few. "Thank you for this, I wouldn't have had time to eat."

"No problem, I just wanted to ask you a few more questions and bounce an idea or two off you."

"Me? I don't mind answering your questions, but I'm hardly an expert on criminals. I'd love to ask you a few questions, though."

"About the case?"

She nodded hopefully.

"I can't discuss any open cases that are currently under investigation, I'm afraid. But if it's a question about something that was already released in the press conference, that should be okay."

"Tess and I don't like the fiancé," Kallie stated bluntly. "You remember my friend Tess Russo, right? We think that James Davis guy is really creepy. Anyone could tell he wasn't upset at the press conference, and it's his own bride-to-be that was murdered. Are you checking him out?"

"We're checking everyone out, Miss Brooks," Morrison replied simply. "But he's not our primary suspect, and he's cooperating fully with our investigation."

"What about the landlord? Have you found him?" Kallie asked, sounding a little hostile even to her own ears. She tried to tone down her attitude a little. "I mean, who just leaves town like that?"

"We've contacted him, and he's on his way back to Florida now. I can't really discuss much more about him, but he didn't break any laws by leaving town. We'll be releasing more information about him when he returns to Sarasota. That's out of my jurisdiction, but their local police have been very helpful so far."

Kallie nodded, appeased for the moment that the detective was telling her all he could.

"I wanted to ask you about your parking place that night," Morrison began his own questions. "Do you always park so far from the door, where the cameras can't reach?"

Kallie was a little insulted, but she decided that it seemed like a valid question. "No, it was only because it was a Saturday night during the height of Spring Break, and the whole lot was packed when I got there. I think we went over this that night."

"We did, I just wanted to refresh my memory. It's unfortunate that the cameras cover so much of the bar and exterior but missed your car."

"I thought that was why the murderer picked my car." *Wait, does he think I'm involved? Like I left my car in the shadows for the killer?*

"That's a very real possibility. And it was blocked from the streetlights by the overhanging trees, too. Not that there are very many streetlights in that area."

Kellie nodded. Owhiro was a quirky and old-fashioned town in a lot of ways, one of which was a lack of garish, ugly modern light posts. The only public lighting near the beach was supplied by antique-style street lamps with round tops, which were popular for their cute, nostalgic design, but not very illuminating.

They were reaching the end of the walkway and nearing her house. "Have you been able to clear Mike yet?" she asked nervously.

"Not yet. We haven't been able to find anyone who can verify why he was outside the bar, and outside of the camera views, for so long." He paused for a moment and added, "It's not that we suspect he's the murderer, Miss Brooks. But he had plenty of time to circle the building to the parking lot. And with so many outdoor cameras, it's odd that he just disappeared."

"I see. Well, I can tell you this: it wasn't him."

Morrison nodded but didn't reply.

"You don't believe me," Kallie added, getting annoyed. "But I've known him for years, and he wouldn't hurt a fly. Much less a helpless girl."

She knew Detective Morrison had heard all of her pleas before, from a thousand different people, about a thousand different suspects. And half of those suspects were probably killers in the end.

I don't have any proof that he's innocent, she thought to herself. *Just my gut instinct. And how many of the others, who insisted their friends were innocent, had to eventually face the fact that they were wrong? That they were fooled too?*

And yet, she couldn't stop herself.

"Mike's just not that kind of person. I'm telling you, he didn't do it."

Chapter Nine

"I'm so annoyed that your boyfriend isn't looking into that poor girl's shady fiancé," Tess complained that evening after work.

"Okay, first of all, Detective Morrison isn't my boyfriend—"

"He took you to dinner."

"He didn't take... He bought me gummy bears, Tess." Her friend grinned, and Kallie rolled her eyes. "Forget it. He told me the fiancé is cooperating, so he has to start looking at other suspects. If they harass him, the slimy creep will hire a lawyer and the police will get sued or something."

"But even I can tell that guy's guilty, Kallie."

"Yeah, he's not exactly trying to make himself look innocent and grief-stricken, is he?"

"I mean, he could have at least *tried* to look sad, especially when he was on camera in front of the whole world. How can they possibly think not he's the killer? It's much more likely to be him than the landlord."

"Definitely," Kallie agreed. "I do think it's weird that the landlord left town right after his tenant was murdered, though."

Tess sipped her beer while Kallie nursed a tall, icy lemonade. The blistering late-spring heat hadn't broken yet, and the summer rains were still holding off near the coast. It was only bearable to sit on the patio on evenings like this one.

"Who else is the detective looking at?" Tess asked.

"I don't know. He can't tell me, remember? Probably the landlord." She laughed as Tess smirked at that. "You don't really think he's my boyfriend, right?"

Her best friend nodded resignedly. "I wish he was, though. He's cute."

"I guess," she grumbled. "I'd think he was cuter if he'd stop talking about Mike and focus on the bad guys."

"Like the landlord?" Tess circled back, jokingly.

"Maybe. At least if it's the landlord, we can be pretty sure Morrison will catch him," Kallie agreed with certainty.

"When he gets back to Florida, you mean? In the meantime, what are the police even doing, right now? I know Owhiro is a tiny little town, and they have to protect big St Petersburg, where people get murdered all the time, but—"

"He *did* come up here—"

"You said he came up here for *another* case, not for Alexandra's case."

"That's true..." Kallie replied, seeing her point.

"The story's all over the news, but is anyone actually working on it? Here, in Owhiro?"

"I've been wondering the same thing, actually. It doesn't seem any closer to being solved." She watched a trio of birds playing on the lakeshore for a moment, then took a deep breath and continued, "I didn't want to worry you, but I've been having nightmares. I thought they'd stop, but they haven't..."

"Kallie! You should've told me!"

"And I may have had a *tiny* panic attack—"

"What?!"

"In the bathtub."

"Okay, that's it. You're coming to stay with me."

Kallie laughed awkwardly, "Then I'll have a panic attack about my dad being home alone."

"Of course you will," Tess replied, gently.

"Anyway, in the nightmares, Lex is reaching out and begging me for help. At first, I just thought it was scary, because she was faceless and wild, but now I'm starting to feel like—"

"Like you should help her," Tess finished her sentence.

"Yeah. And it would really help both her and me, because I don't think I'm going to sleep until this is solved. And like you said, it doesn't seem like anyone else is working on it."

"Okay, well, I'm sleeping here tonight, so the killer will have to get through me *and* Sherman to get to you. And in the morning, we'll start looking for a way to help Lex."

* * * * *

Kallie woke up when her alarm went off at 7:30 the next morning, stunned to find that she really did sleep better with Tess in the house. She threw on a fuzzy robe and walked out of her bedroom to find Tess and Sherman snuggled up on the couch.

"Hey, Kal. How'd you sleep?"

"Better, thanks to you. What are you two doing?"

"I'm researching our primary suspect, and Sherman is helping me by nudging my hand for a treat every time I try to type."

Sherman smiled up at Kallie and wagged his tail, as if verifying that this was indeed a very helpful trick.

"There's coffee in the kitchen, and I started a batch of blueberry muffins. They should be almost ready. Then come see what I found."

Kallie came back a few minutes later with a cup of coffee and two hot muffins. Handing one over, she sat down to see what Tess was doing.

"So I found the fiancé's full name, which luckily is less common than James Davis. Can you believe his middle name is Broderick Alastair? James Broderick Alastair Davis?

"Wow," Kallie replied. "He didn't look like the type. How did you even find that?"

"I looked up their wedding registry."

"Oh my gosh, Tess. You are so freakin' smart!"

"Don't you dare tell anyone," she joked. "From there it was pretty easy to find his social media."

"I bet!"

"I actually tried that first, but there are twenty million guys named James Davis, so I needed his full name." She opened one of the popular platforms and pointed to a pair of seemingly duplicated pages. "The funny thing is, there are two accounts for James Broderick Alastair Davis. One's public, where he has all his photos with Lex and their families. But the other account is private. It's obviously the same guy, and I'm betting that's where he keeps his dirty secrets."

"Would he put his secrets online?"

"Probably not about the murder, although he wouldn't be the first monster to livestream something heinous. But about his slimy personal life, I'd wager money on it."

By the time they'd checked out all of the public posts they could find, it was almost nine a.m., and they both needed to get ready for work.

"This whole 'having a job' thing is really cutting into our sleuthing time," Kallie complained. "I really think we're onto something, Tess. I wish we could keep looking."

"Well luckily, I'm not that busy at work right now. Winchester's going on vacation next week, out of town, and he doesn't want any new cases until he gets back. I'll see what I can find online when I'm not busy chasing away new business."

"You have such a weird job."

"Weird but fun," Tess replied with a laugh.

* * * * *

"Wait, what?" Kallie coughed out a laugh, when Tess came over that night for dinner and announced how she'd spent the afternoon. "You hacked his social media account?"

"Don't make it sound so clandestine. I didn't *hack* his account, I just figured out his password."

"You should've replaced all of his posts with Hello Kitty pictures!"

Tess grinned. "I thought about it, but it's safer to just be quiet about it and look around. I actually took screenshots of everything, because I expected him to change his password by now. But I guess he lets those 'unknown login warning' emails go to his spam folder."

"Oops," Kallie replied with a laugh while she stirred the spaghetti on the stove.

"And really, if your password is 'Password123', then you deserve to be hacked," Tess mumbled in annoyance.

"It doesn't look much like his public account, does it?" Kallie noted, taking a moment to look at the laptop screen.

"Not a single picture of Lex here, I already checked."

"I expected to see something really seedy, but it looks like it's all about money. Fancy cars, big houses. Is that a Lear jet?" Kallie rolled her eyes. "Doesn't he know that even the Royals fly commercial now?"

"Let me find one post in particular, where he was talking to some guy about getting rich, too."

Tess scrolled down until she found a post with a photo of a flashy red sports car. "I had a lot of time to read, with the phones being basically off-limits at work. Check this out."

She slid the laptop over to Kallie, so she could read the conversation in the comments.

Player123: *How's it going with that rich girlfriend of yours?*

JDMoney: *She's my fiancée now, man. So it's going great, lol.*

Player123: *Just as long as you can get her to elope and skip the pre-nup.*

JDMoney: *I don't think her dad will go for that, bro. But it'll be a good ride for as long as I can keep her. If I invest whatever I can get from her, then I can afford to live on that after she kicks me out.*

Player123: *You're like a kid with an allowance.*

JDMoney: *Exactly, dude! Haha!*

"So he really was after Alexandra's money," Kallie groaned. "He must've gotten greedy, or desperate. If he knew she wouldn't marry him without a pre-nuptial agreement, maybe he snapped."

"You know, that's not completely crazy. If he was frantic for money, and managed to get away with killing her, I'll bet he could sue the city for negligence in her murder. And maybe even get part of her life insurance."

"Whoa."

"Or, he could have just been an ordinary greedy, freeloading gold-digger."

"Yeah. Either way, he's a jerk."

* * * * *

The cicadas chirped loudly as Tess and Kallie sat

on the patio later that night, both sipping iced tea. Tess was silently reading from her phone – neither of them mentioned what both of them were thinking.

Finally, Tess gave in. "So the shady fiancé lives in Clearwater, apparently."

"Oh yeah?" Kallie answered, as nonchalantly as possible, though her heart was beating a tiny bit faster.

"Near the hospital. Or so the internet says." Tess pointed at the screen of her phone.

They both kept their eyes on the lake, sitting calmly, as if they were discussing the weather.

"That's a really long way from Lex's place in Sarasota."

"Yep."

"It's pretty close to here, actually."

"Yep."

"Wouldn't take more than twenty minutes to reach the Clearwater hospital from here. If someone needed a hospital, you know. Pretty quick."

"Mmm-hmm," Tess nodded.

The patio went silent again, except for the screech of night insects and the occasional loud call of a passing heron. Tess shook the remaining ice in her glass and crunched a half-melted cube quietly.

"Are you thinking what I'm thinking?"

"Mmm-hmm," Tess nodded again.

They sat quietly for a few more minutes, watching the lights come on in a few houses along the water, as the evening grew darker. Tess crunched another ice cube patiently.

"So are we doing this?" Kallie finally turned to look at her best friend, who was smirking back at her knowingly.

"I'll get my keys."

* * * * *

"Tell me the truth. When we were in high school, did you ever picture us sitting in a car, in the suburbs, in the dark, drinking Mountain Dew to stay awake and stalking a possible murderer?"

"You had me right up until the 'possible murderer' part," Tess admitted.

Kallie laughed. "Stalking Josh Mendoza, maybe?"

"Yes, in a car, in the dark, stalking Josh Mendoza — definitely! And his friend..."

"Daniel something. Yeah, football player, but smart and brooding."

"Yeah." They both thought about their high school crushes for a fleeting moment. "But *not* a possible murderer. We were never this stupid, not even in high school."

"I certainly didn't picture us both single, and me living with my dad," Kallie added.

"Hey, speak for yourself. I'm happily divorced," Tess retorted. "Besides, I love your dad."

"Yeah, he's much nicer than any of the boneheads I dated. And he vacuums."

They watched the empty driveway for a few more minutes, sipping their caffeine-laden sodas. They had driven out to the house in Clearwater on a lark, just to see if they could catch James Davis in some kind of— Kallie didn't even know what they thought he might be doing. But the longer they sat in the car, the more serious it became in her mind.

"Do you think he really killed her?" Tess asked softly, echoing her own thoughts.

"My dad?" she joked, awkwardly.

"I'm serious, Kallie. This guy might really have killed that poor girl. I mean, she was practically a kid. She's my niece's age." There was still no one at the house, but Tess stared out of the car window like she was seeing the young, doomed couple under the streetlight.

"Morrison doesn't think so."

"Do you?"

Kallie turned and looked at her friend, unsure of what to say. She decided on the truth. "Yeah, I do. At the press conference, he wasn't crying and didn't really even talk about Lex at all." She knew that wasn't enough to make him guilty. "I know everyone handles a tragedy differently, but he didn't even seem surprised."

"Did Morrison tell you why he wasn't in custody?"

"No, but he said the creep was 'cooperating'," she replied with the accompanying air-quote finger-gestures. "That usually means 'not a suspect'."

"And yet, here we are. I still think he's the killer, too, for the record. But I'm surprised you're second-guessing the detective."

"It's just a feeling," Kallie shrugged. "Just my gut. Which is getting hungry, by the way. Did you buy anything besides caffeine?"

"But of course, Miss Poirot." Tess reached into the back seat and pulled out two fabric grocery bags. They had stopped for gas on the way, and Tess had apparently done a little shopping inside the station. "Oreos, Twix, Pecan Sandies, economy-size Rice Crispy Treats," she recited, checking the first bag. "Peanut M&Ms, and gummy bears, of course."

"Is that all?" Kallie asked sarcastically.

Tess gasped in mock horror, and snatched the other bag into her lap. "Cool Ranch Doritos!" she snapped. "Pretzel sticks, cheddar and sour cream potato chips, Wheat Thins, everything bagel chips, garlic pita crisps, sriracha cashews, and teriyaki beef jerky."

"Dang, girl."

"And chocolate-covered bacon. In case you can't decide."

"Seriously?"

Tess waggled a colorful bag in front of Kallie's face.

"ChocoPork? That's disgusting."

Tess raised an expectant eyebrow.

"And yet strangely enticing. Gimme."

* * * * *

"Is that him?" Tess whispered, peeking out of the car window into the sweltering suburban darkness.

"I guess so."

They'd been sitting in Tess's car for over an hour, since Kallie's yellow rental car was too obvious, waiting for the victim's fiancé to get home. After endless snacks and singing along with the radio – lights off but air conditioning on – a strange car had finally pulled into the driveway.

Tess squinted in his direction. "I expected him to be taller. And better looking."

"How can you tell if he's good-looking? It's dark."

"I don't know, he's just—"

"Crap, he saw us!" They both ducked down into their seats, and then realized they were being much more obvious by ducking, and sat back up.

"What are we even doing here?" Tess asked. They hadn't really planned this far ahead, and now they had the presumed killer in their sights. "We can't just ask him if he killed her."

"Okay, yeah, let's think of something..."

"Maybe we can ask to borrow his jumper cables, and then he'll open his trunk!"

"His *trunk*?"

"And he'll have the murder weapon in there! And we'll catch him!"

"You've lost your mind, Tess."

"Well, he might have something in there. A bloody tarp, at least. Or her real clothes?"

Kallie gave that some thought, and looked at Tess sideways. "Maybe. Do you really want to try it?"

"Seriously? *What if he's a killer?!*"

"It was your idea!"

"Oh, right. Sure, okay, we outnumber him, and he has no reason to think we're suspicious of him."

"Except the fact that we've been sitting here staring at him for ten minutes."

"Yeah, except that."

When they looked back, though, the driveway

was empty again. "Well now he's parked the car and gone inside the house." Kallie sulked, "We missed our only chance. We should just go home."

"Yeah, probably," Tess replied, disappointed. "Hey, did you just hear a click?"

"No," Kallie answered, with her mouth full of Doritos.

"Stop crunching for a second, I think I heard a click."

"A click like a ballpoint pen? Or a click like a gun?" she asked, swallowing hard.

"*Shhh.* I heard it again. Is your window down?"

"I don't think so." Kallie pushed the automatic window button, and the window rolled up half an inch. It was shockingly noisy in the silence. "Oh, gosh, it *was* down a little." *Oops.*

"The noise must've been outside the car. You didn't hear it?" Suddenly a bright flash lit up the car windows, blinding them both momentarily.

"What was *THAT?!*"

As Tess's vision recovered, she suddenly saw a strange man outside in the dark, only about three feet away. There was another flash.

"It's that guy! He's taking pictures of us!"

"What? WHY?! Owww! My eyes. *Stop it!*" Kallie yelled. It was too dark to see anything but the man's outline, and the camera flash was making it even worse.

Tess yanked the door open and confronted the guy before he could take another shot. "What's *wrong* with you?!"

"*Me*?!" he yelled. "You're the one that's been sitting in this car for two hours. What are *you* doing? I should call the cops."

"We're *helping* the cops, you jerk!" Kallie snarled at him – silently amending her statement with '*secretly* helping' in her head. "Did you think of *that*, before you made a big public scene?"

"Yeah, you probably chased away our suspect," Tess yelled across to the open door.

"Jimmy's your suspect? What'd he do?" the stranger asked. *Jimmy? Wait, this guy knows Alexandra's fiancé?*

"We can't discuss ongoing cases," Kallie replied, now crunching on a pretzel. That's what the police always said on TV, and she'd heard it plenty of times from Morrison himself, recently. "What can you tell us about Jimmy?"

* * * * *

"Wait, *what?*" Tess gasped, confused, ten minutes later.

Kallie and Tess had convinced the neighbor to get into the backseat of their 'undercover' car, where they could see him, and he was telling them all of the local gossip on the fiancé. They couldn't have asked for a better snitch.

"Jimmy has another girlfriend, that's what I'm saying!"

"Hang on. So he's engaged to this beautiful, rich, generous girl. Crazy rich. And he's seeing someone else?" Kallie asked.

"I knew he was slimeball," Tess muttered.

"She's an ex-girlfriend of his, from college or something. She's gorgeous, if I'm being honest." His eyes went a little unfocussed and dreamy at the thought of Jimmy's secret girlfriend. "I didn't know Alexandra Clemons – I've only seen her picture on the news – but this girl is the opposite of her. She's tall, and she has long, curly black hair. And she has this *walk—*"

"Ahem," Tess shook him back into the real world.

"Anyway, she's always broke," he resumed his gossip thread. "She comes around asking him for money, and when I see them together, they're usually both drunk. They fight like cats and dogs, so the whole street knows when she's here."

"And *was* she here?" Kallie asked. "The day the Owhiro Murder happened?"

"Ohhh yeah," he answered with a caustic laugh, shaking his head. "She was here all afternoon. They had a legendary fight that day. She knocked the mailbox over with a baseball bat and tried to smash the garage door down too. Jimmy had to call the police, and then they spent the whole evening with the cops. It was a zoo around here."

Kallie looked over at Tess and shook her head. So that's why Morrison wasn't investigating the fiancé. You can't get a much better alibi than hanging out with the police all night.

Chapter Ten

The next night, they were back at Kallie's house – playing cards with her dad. Tess still insisted on sleeping in the guest room, and she even stopped at her house for a suitcase of clothes.

The disappointment from their first official investigation into the Owhiro Murder was completely forgotten, and they were already moving on to the next possible suspect.

"Hey Tess, which blogger had the photo of my car that night?"

"It was the female one," Tess replied, without looking up from her cards.

"That narrows it down," Kallie replied sarcastically with a laugh.

"No, I think there's really only one female crime blogger in Tampa. I started reading her blog when that serial killer was on the loose." Tess thought for minute. "I think her name's Helen. Or Haley."

Kallie scrolled through the search page on her computer but didn't find anything.

"Are you sure?"

"Yeah. Haley, I think. Or, wait no, it's Hannah."

Kallie tried the search again and found her. "Hannah, that's her. Let's see if she has more information now. Detective Morrison is obviously too busy and too far away from Owhiro. And I'm getting tired of stalking this killer alone."

"Hey! I've been a perfectly good co-stalker," Tess retorted.

"True, but we need help."

Kallie's dad threw down his remaining cards gleefully. "Ha, gin!" He always killed them both at high stakes gin rummy.

Tess gave up her poker chips and joined Kallie at the laptop. A moment later, her dad joined them too.

"Is that the house she rented?" he asked, pointing at the blogger's photo on her screen. "Her landlord was on the news today."

"Was he?" Kallie switched on the television, knowing the local 24-hour news channel would be on an hourly loop until the ten p.m. anchors came on. "I want to see what he says."

It turned out he didn't say much, although he made some rude gestures. The police had mentioned that the landlord would be coming back to Florida, and about thirty reporters were waiting for him like vultures.

After he drove slowly and carefully through the

crowds clustered around his shop, they immediately swarmed his car when he pulled into a parking space. *Surely there's another contingent waiting at his house, and probably another at the rental house,* Kallie thought, without much sympathy. *He might as well face them in a public place.*

Kallie would have felt sorry for him, surrounded by a pack of hungry jackals, if he wasn't acting so devious.

A pretty brunette reporter stepped into the television frame, adjusting her earpiece. It had been recorded earlier in the day, and the sun was still shining brightly on her hot pink blouse. "As you can see over my shoulder," she told the camera, "Harvey Keaton has finally returned to Florida, after he famously disappeared following a police interview."

Kallie and Tess couldn't see much over her shoulder except a sea of well-dressed people with microphones.

"Keaton is the landlord of murder victim Alexandra Clemons, and owner of a popular antique store in this Sarasota shopping center. He allegedly went out of town on a completely normal shopping trip to re-stock his store, but after he left, his alibi for the night of the murder was determined to have a few gaping holes in it."

"Ohhh," Tess and Kallie both reacted in unison, while Kallie's dad just shook his head in disgust.

"No wonder the police wanted him to come back," Kallie added, feeling her faith in humanity crumbling. "This poor girl was just surrounded by creepy, devious, awful people."

Behind the reporter, they could see Keaton, the landlord, yelling and gesturing silently at the crowd from inside his car, and then he finally gave up and drove away — just as the police were arriving to break up the mayhem.

* * * * *

"Oh my goodness, I need a drink," a pretty brunette murmured as she dropped onto a barstool in front of Kallie, the next afternoon.

"That's what I'm here for," she smiled. "What can I get you?"

"A divorce attorney and a glass of chardonnay?"

"I'll be right with you on the latter, not so much with the former." She poured a glass of wine and slid it in front of the visibly stressed-out young woman.

Kallie's customer thanked her but only took a sip of her wine, even though she looked like she wanted to guzzle the whole glass. "It's not really that bad. My husband's just being dumb, not divorce-worthy. We own a small restaurant in Clearwater, and I asked him to fire one of the waiters. This guy got drunk and picked

104

a fight with my husband last night."

"Doesn't seem like he'd need encouragement to fire the guy," Kallie noted, quizzically.

"That's exactly what I said!" she replied with a shrug. "But he insists that the guy's a great server and the customers love him."

Kallie nodded. She knew what she'd do with a drunk, aggressive waiter – especially in her current stressed-out frame of mind since the murder. *More drama, no thanks!*

Still, she didn't feel ready to inject her uninformed opinion into this personal subject. *Man, working the day shift is a lot more complicated than the night shift*, she thought to herself. *My night folks just wanted loud music, a beer, and maybe a dozen wings — they didn't want to talk about their life issues.*

"But who cares if the customers like him? If he hates my husband, he's out, right?" the woman continued. Luckily, she didn't wait for Kallie's response. "But Felix insists the guy's worth keeping. And, I mean, he gets along fine with *me,* so I guess I should just let him deal with it. But what happens if his bad temper spills over onto the customers?"

This time she paused for input, so Kallie offered, "So he was drunk at work?"

She was deflecting, but it seemed like a valid point. Kallie felt like she should order a Psychology 101 textbook when she got home.

"Exactly! He had finished his shift, but he can't just come back to work drunk and pick fights!"

Kallie nodded, certain she'd be fired if she ever did that, but she kept her mouth shut. *Maybe a Psychology 201 book. And another deep chat with Amelia and Marcy.*

"Are you new?" the young woman finally asked.

"Not really, I've worked on the night shift for years. I recently started working days, though. I'm Kallie."

"Josie," the young woman shook her hand over the wine glass. "My husband Felix and I like to meet here after our lunch shift ends, since we live in Owhiro. He'll be here soon."

Kallie reminded herself to stay as far away as possible from that conversation.

* * * * *

When Kallie looked up from serving drinks to other customers an hour later, she noticed that the young woman who had introduced herself as Josie and her husband were arguing quietly over their potato skins at a nearby table. That was another pleasant change from her experience on the night shift.

Plenty of couples fought with each other at the Lazy Gecko during the night shift, but almost none of them were quiet and polite about it.

"The guy made one mistake, Josie," she heard Felix explain. "It was a doozy, I'll admit, but he's reliable and the customers love him."

"I don't know how you can say that—"

"Have you seen our reviews online? Half of the five-star reviews mention him by name. Apparently he's 'funny and knowledgeable,' and an expert on the wine selection. As well as 'super cute,' since that's obviously relevant in a restaurant review."

Josie slumped back in her seat, trying not to laugh. "I mean, it's your call. You're the one who has to deal with him."

"I've really just always liked him. I know you spend more time with the chefs than the wait staff, but he's a good guy. He's smart and he's never late, and he's been with us for almost seven months. Longer than anyone else on that shift."

"Okay, okay, I get it. I hope he knows how much you're sticking your neck out for him," she grumbled. "I would've kicked his butt to the curb."

"You would've called the cops," he replied with a laugh.

"Actually, that's true. If I'd been there alone when it happened, I *would've* called the cops."

The smile slid from his face, and they both sat in silence for a moment, obviously thinking about her level of worry behind that statement.

"Do you really want me to fire him, Jojo?"

"No," she sighed. "I love you even more for giving him a second chance. But please keep an eye on him. Like a silent probation period?"

"You got it, baby."

Kallie smiled to herself, while quietly watching the young couple from the bar. *Maybe I won't need that psychology textbook after all.*

Chapter Eleven

Going to work before noon was still throwing off Kallie's internal clock, but she was starting to like the regular customers. If she didn't stop eating the amazing lunch food, though, she was going to gain twenty pounds. She still wasn't making enough money to pay her bills, but at least Marcy didn't charge her for the food. And she loved being home in the evenings, so she got a chance to actually see her father and her dog while they were awake.

Tonight she was snuggling with Sherman on the couch and cyber-stalking the local crime bloggers. Two of them were particularly talented at finding sources and leaks, and she wanted to ask them for their help, so she started investigating them first.

"Clearwater Crime" was the most popular, hosted by a writer called Sherlock1104. The fact that Clearwater was in the blog's name probably meant that he wasn't too far away, but there was no contact email address or automated form. Kallie really needed to talk to him directly, and she couldn't exactly go door-to-door through the whole city. Scouring through the blog archives, she found references to a few restaurants and coffee shops where he liked to hang out. There were a few very old photos of him, and it seemed like his real name might be John. After twenty minutes of browsing, though, she decided she couldn't just wait in a coffee shop for days with these few clues, ready to pounce if he ever showed up. With no other way of reaching out to him, she left what she hoped was an intriguing comment on his latest blog post and gave up.

Her next option was "Homicide in Paradise," written by the woman named Hannah whom Tess had recommended, and who appeared to live in downtown Tampa. She had a lot of photos in her blog posts, including the first shots of Kallie's car in the Lazy Gecko's dark parking lot. Recent updates sounded like she had a good source within the police station, too. Kallie definitely needed to talk to Hannah, who luckily had a 'tip line' email address on her blog. She sent a message explaining who she was and asking to chat.

Those were the only locals who seemed well-connected enough to risk contacting, so Kallie snapped her laptop shut and went to fix dinner for Sherman and herself. Her father said he wasn't hungry, but she knew she could tempt him with homemade tuna casserole. Boiling the noodles, she wondered absently who Hannah's contact within the police might be. She didn't share any details that would be illegal or risky, but she knew a lot more specifics of the case than Kallie did. *Could she be dating an officer? Or maybe she was secretly be a cop herself, masquerading behind a pseudonym online? Surely not.*

She'd have to wait and find out from the source — Kallie was pretty sure she could entice the blogger to talk to her, if not meet in person. She and Tess might not have found the right murder suspect yet, but Hannah didn't know that. And Kallie had a few juicy bits of information to share, which she was sure Hannah could use to intrigue her readers.

* * * * *

Putting the laptop back on a shelf of the dining room sideboard, she called Sherman to eat his dinner, which included a few bites of tuna tonight. Sherman was a rescue, taken as a puppy from an abusive hoarding situation, and Kallie had nurtured him from a scared, untrusting waif into a happy fuzzball.

He woke up from his nap and ran, wagging all over, to the kitchen to meet her. He could be pretty stoic, but not when she'd been gone all day. He wasn't quite accustomed to her working the day shift yet, so seeing her in the evenings was still a thrill.

Kallie pulled a secret Milk Bone from her pocket and asked for a high five, snuggling him when he complied. "Good boy!"

"You're spoiling him," her dad called from the table, where he had indeed been lured by the smell of the baking casserole.

"This from you, who feeds him bacon from your own plate?" she called back with a grin.

"Only when I make too much," he tried to reply innocently.

"Don't listen to him!" she told Sherman. "You deserve to be spoiled."

* * * * *

After dinner, Kallie went out to check the mail, since the evening had cooled down a bit. She was walking back to the house when a small, round woman with coke-bottle glasses and electric salmon-orange hair accosted her.

"Kalliope dear!" she shrieked, as Kallie backpedaled away from her.

"Mrs. Jones! Where did you come from?!"

"I was hiding in— I mean, I was just walking past the hedges. I'm very petite, you know. You must've missed me."

Mrs. Jones might have been short, but she wasn't petite. Kallie somehow resisted the urge to tell her that.

"I brought a lemon meringue pie for your father, dear. I'll just take it inside to him. It needs to pop back in the fridge, you know." The little fireplug tried to elbow her way past Kallie, but she didn't make it to the stairs.

"I'm afraid he's napping and can't be disturbed, Mrs. Jones." Kallie was much taller and could see through the front window – her father was waving his arms frantically and trying to find a place to hide.

Snatching the pie from the older woman's clutches, she dashed up the stairs, yelling, "I'll let him know you stopped by!"

* * * * *

"Do you think I'm being too hard on them?" Kallie had asked Tess once, after chasing two of the horrible women off the front lawn.

"No way, Kal. They're vultures," her best friend had replied sincerely.

"Do you think so?"

"They don't even like your dad. They just show up like scavengers, competing with each other and looking for fresh meat. They're awful."

"But they're little old ladies."

"Don't you fall for that. If your dad meets a nice lady that he likes, I promise he'll let you know. He definitely won't be hiding in the pantry."

"That's a good point," Kallie agreed with a laugh.

"In the meantime, they can keep bringing

dessert. Let's encourage the redhead who brought that amazing key lime pie last week."

"You got it."

"Just make sure your dad's not home. She might be a vulture, but she's a great cook."

* * * * *

Kallie woke up early the next morning and couldn't go back to sleep. Knowing she'd soon start to worry if she sat there awake in the dark, she instead crept out to the dining room for her laptop and carried it back to bed.

"Hi Kallie," the short email read, "sounds like an interesting offer. Can you meet for coffee in downtown Tampa today?"

Kallie hadn't expected such a quick, if brief, reply from Hannah, and she wasn't sure if she could manage a meeting with her new work schedule. However, curiosity quickly got the better of her.

It was only 7:30 a.m. when she came back inside from walking Sherman, and she answered the email before she even opened her first diet coke of the morning. She had to be at work early, so she replied to Hannah that she could meet at 9:00 a.m., suggesting a local spot near the highway. She still needed to shower and change and grab a bite to eat, and she'd be cutting it a little close.

By 8:15 a.m. she was out the door and hoping she'd miss morning traffic. It would take at least half an hour to get to downtown Tampa, and she still had to find parking.

Luckily there wasn't much traffic on the bridge, and she made good time, walking into Brew Ha-Ha Cafe just a minute before nine. She knew the owners from a few local events that they both attended for work, and waved hello to them as she looked for someone who might be Hannah. She hadn't thought to ask the blogger for a description of herself. Seeing a serious-looking blonde in her early thirties with a notepad and pen in her lap, typing on a laptop, she approached on a hunch.

"Hannah?"

The blonde looked up, took off her glasses, and seemed to consider her options for a moment. "Kallie?"

Kallie started to sit down, but Hannah stood up quickly. "I needed this table space to catch up on work, but let's go sit in the back where it's quieter."

She had apparently scoped out the place before Kallie arrived, and led the way back to a pair of overstuffed chairs near the kitchen door. Kallie didn't normally drink gourmet coffee but took the rare opportunity to order a big, slushy, frozen caramel-coffee concoction with whipped cream. It probably didn't make her look stoic, daring, or professional, but she really didn't think it mattered. Hannah would either agree to her collaboration idea or not.

"So you work at the Lazy Gecko?" Hannah asked, without a second glance at Kallie's decadent drink choice.

"Yes, and I worked the night shift until recently."

"So you were there the night Alexandra Clemons was killed?"

"I... Actually..." she knew her stammering made it sound like she was lying, but she hadn't discussed that evening with any strangers. *What exactly did you think was going to happen here today, Kallie? If you don't tell her, she can't help you.*

She suddenly thought she might cry and struggled to fight it off. "Actually, they found her in *my car.*"

Chapter Twelve

"So, let me get this straight," Hannah mused. "You didn't actually see anything that night, and you don't even have the car back yet?" She seemed both suspicious and slightly annoyed. *She thinks I'm lying – or just wasting her time. I hope she's not right...*

"I did see her," Kallie corrected the blogger. "I just thought she was trying to carjack me or something. One of our bouncers was the one who figured out the whole... situation."

"Mike, right?"

"Yeah. Did you talk to him?"

"No, I tried to interview him, but he wouldn't talk to me. Carlos either."

Kallie wondered if they were protecting Marcy, and she smiled a little. *They could've made good money giving interviews,* she thought. *If Alexandra was surrounded by monsters, I'm surrounded by the nicest guys ever.*

"I *don't* have my car back, yet, though. They keep saying 'one more day.'"

"So you don't have the car, and you don't have a first-hand account, but you want to share the credit?"

Hannah asked, raising an eyebrow.

"Not the credit," Kallie replied quickly. "I just want to share the details." She blushed a little, then sucked up her courage and admitted, "To be honest, I really just want to find the killer."

"Oh, is *that* all?" Hannah laughed.

"I have some information from the lead detective on the case, and I've been doing research with my best friend." She thought for a minute — did she have anything else to offer? It was starting to sound like she really was just wasting Hannah's time. "I might be able to get Mike and Carlos to talk to you."

"That would be helpful." Hannah tapped her pen on the table for a few seconds, looking at Kallie like she wanted to ask something, but wasn't sure how to word it – and then apparently decided on the direct approach. "I don't mean to be rude, but you know the cops still think Mike might be the killer, right?"

"Yes, I've heard that," Kallie growled, still angry at Detective Morrison for not believing her. "It's not him. I've known him for years."

Hannah nodded ambiguously.

"Let me level with you, Kallie. This conversation would be pointless if it was just a blog post," Hannah said, after looking carefully at her for a moment. "I wouldn't even have met you for coffee, to be perfectly frank. But I'm thinking about writing a book."

"A book? About the Owhiro Murder?"

Hannah nodded. "I'm right here in the middle of the story, and I've been covering it since day one. My daily stats have tripled since her family fortune made the national news. True Crime stories are incredibly popular right now. This is the perfect time."

The whole thing seemed a little mercenary to Kallie, at first thought, but it was really no different than blogging about it. Just more investigation and analysis on Hannah's part. *With a little luck, that extra research and collating might help uncover the killer.*

"Isn't it too soon?"

"The way I figure, the book needs to be ninety-percent written when they catch the killer. That way I can tie up the details and go to press right away. In the meantime, I need as many reliable sources as I can get."

"Does that mean you'll work with me?" Kallie asked, a little surprised.

"If you want to risk your life, that's your problem. But I'll give you a contributor credit on the book if you tell me all you know, and I'll share everything I've found out. Most of my details are already on the blog, but I have a few other leads that I haven't published yet. Sound like a deal?"

Kallie nodded in agreement, reaching over her mostly untouched drink to shake hands. "Deal."

* * * * *

"So the two people who seem the most suspicious to me right now are the landlord and the fiancé," Hannah read from her notebook. "There was a female roommate for a while, but she moved to Fort Myers last year. Just before Thanksgiving. And there's a business partner, but I'm having trouble finding any information about her."

"What do you know about the fiancé? We checked him out, and he seems to have a pretty perfect alibi."

"Does he? My source said he's not the main suspect anymore, but I hadn't heard about an alibi."

Kallie heart jumped so hard when Hannah mentioned her source, she almost missed the rest of the sentence. *So she does have a source within the police department!* This was exactly the reason Kallie had approached the blogger, and she hoped it would bring her some of the details that Morrison couldn't share.

"He's sort of an aging frat boy," Hannah continued, "who thinks he's still the hottest guy in town. Getting a little paunchy after his football days."

"Nice."

"I can't imagine what she saw in him, unless maybe they've been a steady couple since college."

"Since before he was paunchy?" Kallie asked

with a laugh.

"It's not just that. He comes across as a real sleazeball."

"Slimier than you know." Kallie told Hannah briefly about the gossipy neighbor and the alleged mysterious, broke, and angry girlfriend.

"Well, he would never have gotten rich by marrying her, although he could've been in denial about that. Alexandra's family was rich, but she was running a non-profit, so it's not like she was a lovestruck party girl socialite rolling in cash. And there's no way her dad would've let her skip the pre-nup." She took a tablet out of her purse, pulled up a photo, and passed it to Kallie. That was definitely the guy they'd seen in the driveway, but Tess had been right — he'd already lost his looks.

Kallie nodded and took some notes in her own notepad. "And the landlord?"

"He was overcharging her, but I doubt she cared. Her little house is beautiful, and she didn't need the money. But he had the keys and access to her house, and my source said it looks like the attack may have started there."

"Started at her house? I hadn't heard that."

"There was some kind of struggle, and a few items were knocked over. It could be a coincidence. Maybe she has a problematic cat," she added with a shrug. "But there's a sense from the Sarasota cops that it might've started there."

"Oh really?" *Morrison's a sneaky one, leaving out even the mention of a struggle.* "Motive?"

"None that I'm aware of, but the landlord lied about where he was on the night of the murder."

"Really?!" she repeated, louder. *The news reporter said there was a problem with the landlord's alibi, but not that he'd outright lied.*

"He said he was at Gino's Pizzeria in Old Town all evening, but the whole restaurant is on camera. Door to door, every table, parking lot. Even the bathrooms."

"That seems to be the trend," Kallie added. She was glad that the cameras at the Lazy Gecko proved she was innocent, as annoying as it was.

"The Sarasota and St Petersburg police have both watched the whole surveillance video, from open to close. He wasn't there."

"Wow," Kallie replied simply. *Imagine lying to the police about your alibi, in this day and age. He must've been crazy to think he wouldn't be caught.*

"He hasn't clarified his story yet, but I saw he just got back to Florida."

"I went to school with Gino's granddaughter, Nicola. Maybe I'll stop by the restaurant on my day off. We don't talk much anymore, but she won't think it's weird if I'm gossiping about such a hot topic."

Hannah flipped the page in her notepad. "And the roommate. Former roommate. Betty. No, Betsy. I have her contact information, but I haven't been able to catch her on the phone yet." She handed over the tablet again, with another photo of a mousy but cute brunette and her address and phone number. "I don't really have anything on her, so I'm counting on you to update me if you talk to her."

"Of course. Are you kidding? This is all so helpful; I'll be glad to return any information I can find."

"You really think you can find this murderer?"

"I mean, sure, I guess," Kallie blushed. "I feel so guilty, like I should've saved her."

"Oh, no. Don't do that to yourself."

"Anyway, finding her killer is the least I can do."

"Well, don't get yourself killed too." Hannah concluded, putting her laptop, tablet, and paper notebook back into her bag. "Be careful out there." She gave Kallie a tentative hug, and they walked out of the coffee shop.

* * * * *

Kallie was working outside that afternoon, which was much better than working inside. The air conditioner had been out since midnight, and the inside of the Lazy Gecko was like a sauna. Only it didn't smell quite as nice as a sauna.

Marcy had the money to fix it, if she could find a repairman with the parts. Unfortunately, it was the hottest part of spring, before the cooling summer monsoon season started, and the repair companies were swamped. *Nursing homes and day care centers without air conditioning somehow take precedence over bars,* Kallie thought to herself with an ironic laugh as she pulled her auburn hair up into a ponytail to cool off a little.

On Tuesday, the previous day, they had even closed for a few hours after lunch. There were ceiling fans on the patio, but they were only stirring the ninety-five-degree soupy air around like a wooden spoon. Pitchers of ice water melted in minutes, and they didn't have anything cold to eat on the menu. Even most of the regulars drank one beer and conceded defeat.

Today, at least, there was a breeze off the gulf. It was still sweltering, and there wasn't a single drop of rain to help, but the breeze on Kallie's face and the locals' laughter kept her going. Teddy was joined on the patio by his wife, Cecilia – blonde hair in a curly bun and dressed in a neon-bright striped sleeveless sundress. It would have been garish on anyone less dazzling, but her outgoing, cheerful sense of humor and sparkling blue eyes lit up the broiling patio.

"Can I get you two bowls of seafood chowder today, Teddy?" Kallie asked playfully when Cici sat down on one of the outdoor barstools.

"That sounds ghastly, thank you," he smiled back. "I'll take the coldest beer you have, and I think Cici wanted a margarita."

"Rocks or frozen?" she asked the bubbly blonde, who seemed to be twinkling, rather than sweating like the rest of them.

"Frozen please, and no salt."

Kallie served Teddy's beer, which immediately started sweating all over the wooden bar top, but he smiled with relief after the first sip.

"I need to go back inside for more ice. My supply out here is completely melted."

There was no ice maker on the patio, so the bus boys had to bring out her ice supply in plastic bins. She started for the door, but bumped into one of the day shift waiters, whom she hadn't seen all shift. He obviously wasn't serving anyone, since the indoor tables were all abandoned. "Perfect timing. Could you go to the kitchen and get me more ice, please? Like, a *lot* more ice?"

He nodded and turned around, hopefully to run her errand. The fact that she hadn't seen him in the past four hours made her think that was unlikely. He must've found some cool place in the building to hide. Or possibly in his car, with the air conditioner running full blast.

At least the ceiling fans on the patio were functioning. The breeze had died down, and it was the hottest time of the day. She stuck a glass into the melted ice and then rolled it over the back of her neck, below her ponytail. As much as she would've loved to dump the whole glass down the back of her shirt, she was pretty sure that'd be unprofessional.

"I'd love an ice cream cone," Cici mentioned, out of the blue.

"You know, I think we might actually have ice cream. I'm pretty sure there's a hot fudge sundae on the lunch menu." Kallie picked up a menu and scanned the back cover.

"Really?!" Teddy and Cici both smiled and looked at each other, then back at her.

"I don't know where that waiter went, but I don't think he's coming back. Make sure everyone behaves, would you, while I run to the kitchen?" *Not that there's anyone left, except reliable Barry with his notebook and his beer.*

Luckily the electricity was working, it was just the air conditioning that was broken. The ice maker and the freezer were still functional, in the kitchen. Kallie came back out five minutes later with two more buckets of ice and about a quarter of a gallon of vanilla ice cream, all stacked on a utility cart.

"I couldn't find any cones, or any chocolate sauce. It took all of my willpower to walk back out of the freezer, honestly," she added with a laugh. "We don't have root beer, but how about a rum and coke float?"

Cici smiled and clapped her hands like it was Christmas. "That sounds *amazing*."

Kallie took out three big beer mugs and filled them halfway with ice-cold coke from the counter soda gun, adding rum to two of them for her patrons, and then divided up the remaining ice cream between the mugs. She couldn't drink on duty, and she wasn't much of a drinker anyway, but Marcy wouldn't mind her having an ice cream float in this weather. They clinked their heavy glasses together like kids, and sipped their sweet, frosty drinks in the tropical Florida heat.

* * * * *

"I don't know how you can stand it," Cici told Kallie, who was fanning herself with a menu.

"I'm getting used to it," she laughed, "and tomorrow's my day off, so I'll have a chance to recover from my heatstroke." *And hopefully run down to Gino's before they get too busy*, she added to herself.

"When is the A/C getting fixed, do you know?" Teddy asked over his drink.

"Marcy's having trouble finding a repairman who doesn't want her to replace the whole system. It's still almost new, and she doesn't want to get ripped off."

"Well, why didn't you *say* so?" Cici chirped, taking her phone out of her purse. "Our son's roommate works for an air conditioning company. Let me call him."

"Oh, I can't ask..."

"Don't try to stop her, Kallie," Teddy warned. "This woman can magically arrange anything. She's a force of nature."

"But—"

"Nope!" they both snapped at her in unison, as Cecilia dialed her son's number and asked to speak to the roommate. "It's a small company, and it'll be great for their reputation," she seemed to be convincing both Kallie and her son's roommate, who had picked up the phone, at the same time. "If he fixes it, you'll recommend them, right?"

"If he can get us up and running for a fair price, I'm sure Marcy will be okay with that!" Kallie told her. "Let me go get her."

Cici's son and his roommate, with the unfortunate name combination of Tom and Jerry, arrived at the Lazy Gecko twenty minutes later. After much hugging from Cecilia, and a short conversation with Marcy, Jerry took out his tools, wiped the fuchsia lipstick off his cheeks, and inspected the outdoor air conditioning unit. He quickly determined that a huge palmetto bug had gotten into the electrical panel and fried the capacitor, and it only needed a replacement part.

"One more reason to hate those nasty bugs,"

Marcy grimaced.

After a quick check in his company truck, Jerry verified that he had the necessary part on hand. The appropriate paperwork was quickly signed by Marcy, and the air conditioner was fixed and humming again in another twenty minutes. They all cheered happily – even the ever-serious Barry – and Marcy bought them all a round of drinks.

"I can't believe two different companies told me I needed to replace the whole system, and it turned out to be so simple," Marcy fumed. She quickly added a promise, "I'm definitely telling everyone I know how honest you are!"

She thanked Cici again profusely, and then quietly discussed with Jerry how she could help him with a glowing five-star review.

By happy hour, it was just barely cool enough indoors to be bearable – and since it was still sweltering outside, they made their way back inside before the after-work crowd appeared.

* * * * *

That evening at home, Kallie walked out onto the back deck to join her dad, carrying a platter of crackers and cheese and a pitcher of lemonade. After a few minutes of thought, she grudgingly went back inside and got her knitting. It was really too hot to bear having the fluffy pink monstrosity on her lap, but Isabel's baby blanket was almost done, and there wasn't much time left.

"It's nice having you back during the day, kiddo," her dad told her.

"Yeah, it's not really daytime, but at least I'm home in time to see the sunset over the lake. And to see you and Sherman while you're awake."

The house was built in the 1940s and it wasn't fancy, but Kallie loved it, and the lake view was so peaceful. After working at night for so long, she'd forgotten how pretty it could be in the evening. Sherman jumped up onto the chaise with her, and the three of them watched the sunset quietly.

"You seem like you're adjusting to the day shift at work," her dad observed.

"My tips are picking up, at least. Lunch is much busier than I expected, which is good. People are getting to know me, and I have some pretty cool regular customers." She stopped and thought for a second. "I still hope Marcy will move me back to the night shift, though."

"Do you?" her dad asked, knowingly.

Kallie smiled. "Sometimes. Mostly I just need the money. And I miss seeing Mike and Carlos. It's nice to be back on an almost-normal schedule, though."

The deck started to get dark, and she lit a few citronella candles on the side tables — for light, and also to keep the mosquitos at bay.

After a little while, Kallie's dad asked, "Has your mother been able to find Jack?"

"I haven't heard from her again, so she must've found him."

"That's good," he replied neutrally. "Speaking of unpleasant blasts from the past, Joseph called while you were out."

"Joseph?" she asked, surprised. "What did he want?"

"I didn't ask him."

Kallie smiled. Her dad had never liked her ex-boyfriend, and she finally understood why.

"Did you tell him I was dead?"

"I considered it. But he sounded like it might be important."

"I doubt it. I'll call him back in the morning, when he's at work."

"So you don't have to talk long," he chuckled. "Good choice."

Kallie and Joseph had been broken up for about a year, and this was the first time he'd called in about six months. Kallie assumed he'd just seen her name in the paper and was being nosey about the murder. There were certainly worse guys in the world, but he was the type who yelled at cashiers when they didn't have enough pennies in the drawer to give him exact change. She figured she'd dodged a bullet.

"Do we have any more of these crackers?" her dad asked, changing the subject. "They're tasty."

"No, we're running out of everything. I'll go to the real grocery store before work tomorrow, now that I don't need to stop at the 24-hour Stoppe-and-Shoppe at three a.m. anymore."

"No more stale, off-brand corn snacks from the power steering fluid aisle?"

"You can have *fresh* off-brand corn snacks now, dad," she laughed at his banter, feeling so blessed that he never really complained about anything. "Make me a shopping list tonight, would you?"

Chapter Thirteen

"Hi, I'm here to check on my car. They said it would be ready today."

The young lady at the police counter, whom Kallie recognized as the younger sister of a guy in her graduating class, looked at her for a second before realizing who she was. "Oh! Oh, no. I'm sorry, it's not here, Miss Brooks. That whole case is being handled by the county."

"The county?"

"We just don't have the manpower here. I mean, that's a really big case. Your car's down in St Pete." She paused, but apparently didn't think that was a good enough explanation. "They have a real crime lab and stuff."

Kallie nodded, realizing it made sense, and not sure why she hadn't thought of it. Owhiro was a tiny beach town with almost no crime. She wasn't even sure if they had a single real detective.

"Let me call them, and make sure it's ready for you. I'd hate for you to drive all the way down there—"

The girl called the St Petersburg office and talked to someone who was apparently a friend, while

Kallie walked around the quaint little police station. It was as quirky and old-fashioned as the rest of Owhiro. Tourists and visitors were always surprised by the adorable town square filled with colorful, historical bungalows and cobblestone streets, on the edge of the bustling combined metropolis of Tampa and St Petersburg.

Pictures of police chiefs and their era-specific cars, going back to the 1940s, hung on the station walls. In a few older black-and-white photos, officers were pictured with horses. Kallie smiled at the faded old photos in spite of her annoyance about the car – trying not to think about the nightmarish crime that had damaged her trust in her tiny, sweet hometown.

"Your car's ready, Miss Brooks," the young lady called, walking back toward to her. *Her name's Jeannie*, Kallie recalled out of the blue, *Jason's sister*. "They said you can pick it up at the main station in St Pete, any time."

"Thanks," she started to leave but Jeannie stopped her, with a gentle hand on her arm.

"I know you don't know me, Miss Brooks, but we're all so sorry this happened."

"Yeah, me too," Kallie replied with a sad smile.

* * * * *

Kallie was walking through the lobby of the St Petersburg police station, looking up at the signs for directions, when she ran into the one person who could help her. Literally. She smacked right into him, almost knocking herself down. Luckily, he caught her by the arm and kept her on her feet.

"I'm so sorry," she started to apologize. "I wasn't looking where— Detective!"

"Miss Brooks, are you okay?" Detective Morrison asked, looking down at her in a mix of surprise and concern, as if she wasn't the one who'd clumsily collided with *him* at full speed.

"I'm fine, I was just looking for my car."

He smiled at her hesitantly, apparently wondering why she was looking for a car in the lobby of an office building.

"I mean, they told me I could pick up my car today. I thought it would be in Owhiro, but then the receptionist said it would be here."

"Ah, understood," he replied with a smile. "Evidence isn't usually kept at this office, but sometimes there are exceptions. Have a seat and I'll check for you."

Kallie had been hoping this would be a quick errand, so she ran outside and told Tess to park the Banana Barge. Her friend had driven down to St Pete with her, so they could each drive a separate car back home. If it was going to take a while, there was no sense in Tess waiting outside in the heat and wasting gas. That monstrosity wasn't exactly an economy car. They walked back into the police station together just as Detective Morrison was returning to the lobby.

"Your car is still at the evidence lockup, Miss Brooks," he notified her with an apologetic expression. "But it's only a mile from here. I'm sorry for the inconvenience — why don't you let me drive you over there? Maybe I can at least help speed up the process."

"Oh, I don't want to be any—" Kallie suddenly felt a sharp elbow jab into her ribs.

"We'd love that! Thank you so much, Detective!" Tess cooed, unnaturally.

Kallie stared at her friend like she'd been infested with alien spawn, but hesitantly agreed with the offer. "If it's not too much trouble, that *would* be a big help."

"No trouble at all. I'll get my car and meet you out front."

After he walked away, Kallie hissed, "What was *that* about?!"

"What? He's cute."

"Tess, I'm not—"

"Who said anything about *you*?" she asked, with a laugh and a wink. "If you want to ignore the hot, sweet guy with a badge, that's your problem."

Kallie was still blinking in surprise at the bizarre

change in her best friend, while she was being dragged toward the door by the hand.

"And we get to ride in his cool car. Come on!"

* * * * *

When they arrived at the processing department entrance of the smaller evidence station, Morrison got out with Kallie and Tess and walked inside with them. Kallie wouldn't even have known where to park, much less who to talk to, so she was glad to have him there.

"This is Kalliope Brooks," he explained at the counter. "She's here to retrieve her car, which was collected as evidence in a murder."

The officer behind the desk checked her computer and found the record quickly. "Yes, K. Brooks. I see it here, detective. She's in lot two, space forty-three. I'd normally walk her out, since the gates are keycard-protected. Do you want to take her?"

"Sure, I'll walk them out." He waved them on, and the three of them walked back out into the mid-morning heat. "I should warn you," he told Kallie as they walked across the parking lot to a fenced area in the back, "there will probably be some damage inside your car. They usually take small cuttings from the seats and carpets for their lab tests."

"Oh, okay."

"You could try filing a claim, if it's something that you believe could be fixed."

By then, Morrison had opened the fence lock with a key card in his vest, and they entered the evidence lot. With ten-foot tarped fences on all sides restricting the air flow, it was even hotter than the scalding main parking lot. Kallie's head was suddenly spinning, but she wasn't sure if she felt dizzy because of the heat or the sight of her car.

In the daylight, she could see where the rear passenger door had been slashed with the killer's screwdriver, and the raw, ripped metal was just starting to rust. As she walked up and peered in the back window, it looked like a small bomb had gone off inside. The back seat was ripped in several places, with stuffing protruding. It was an old car, but she had cared for it lovingly, and her eyes teared up at the missing chunks of carpet and black smears of fingerprint powder staining every section of the fabric.

Tess quickly moved over to comfort her as Kallie's bottom lip started to tremble. "I mean, I was probably going to sell it anyway," she sniffled. "Because of the bad memory. But—"

"We can fix it up, honey. I'll patch the holes in the seat for you, and I'll bet Mike can fix that gash in the door."

"My poor little car." She turned to Tess, with

tears in her eyes. "We had so many fun times in this car."

"I know, Kal. Don't worry. I'll drive it home, and you can drive the rental. I'll talk to Mike..."

Detective Morrison stood to one side, apparently unsure of what to say. Kallie was sure he'd never seen anyone cry over an old, beat-up evidence car before. He silently handed the keys to Tess, even though that wasn't the proper protocol.

"I'll drive you back to the station so you can pick up your rental car, Miss Brooks." He spoke softly, like a visitor at a funeral, and placed his hand on her shoulder to guide her away.

Tess smiled at the detective and wordlessly nodded her thanks. "Don't worry, honey. We'll fix it."

* * * * *

Kallie headed back toward the freeway from the police station in her ugly, rented Banana Barge. Tess had gone on ahead, so she was planning to go home, even though she wasn't in any mood to be alone.

"It's my day off," she mumbled to herself. "I should do something fun."

Yeah, right. You're in a perfect state to do something fun. Grumpy and sad about her poor little damaged car, she tried not to even think about the dead girl that had been hidden in its back seat. Knowing she wouldn't be cheered up anytime soon, she decided to do something useful instead.

Swerving over to the far-left lane, she took the on-ramp headed south on the freeway, instead of taking the northbound route that would carry her home from St Petersburg.

I'm halfway to Sarasota anyway. And I could use a good pizza.

The day was brilliant and sunny and there wasn't much traffic on the road, so it was the perfect time to take the Sunshine Skyway Bridge south across the bay. The huge bridge, tall enough to allow clearance for massive cruise ships beneath it, had terrified her as a teenager. It was still bizarre to drive up the intimidatingly steep slope, with only the sky in sight, land and water only a memory – but it didn't really scare her anymore.

Sure, just don't think about your car breaking down up here, her traitorous brain whispered to her when she reached the top, making her stomach lurch a little – but then she was driving safely back down on the south side of the bridge. The view of pretty Terra Ceia washed away the last of her discomfort, and she turned up the radio. It was another twenty minutes to Sarasota, so she decided to take the Tamiami Trail, just for the view. The narrow old road could be awful during rush hour, but at midmorning it was a nostalgic, retro ride.

Kallie swung into the Gino's Pizzeria parking lot just after they opened at eleven a.m. and found her former schoolmate Nicola running the restaurant. She was inspecting the immaculate tables with their charming red-and-white checkered tablecloths, making sure everything was spotless for the lunch rush. The place had been popular when they were kids, but now it was practically an institution.

"I'm sorry, we're not quite— *Kallie?"* her old friend recognized her and ran over for a hug. "I haven't seen you in ages!"

"I've been working the night shift and I was never able to get down here. But there's no pizza in Owhiro that can compare to yours!"

They sat down in a booth and chatted for a few minutes about their fathers, who were also friends, and about old classmates from high school. Kallie was trying to think of a subtle way to ask about Lex's landlord, when Nicola actually brought up the murder first.

"Speaking of Owhiro, aren't you still tending bar at the Lazy Gecko?"

"Yep, I've been there for six years. Doesn't it seem like just yesterday, when we were twenty-one and partying there?"

"Some days it seems like yesterday, and some days it seems like a hundred years," Nicola laughed.

"Same here!"

"So were you there when that girl was killed?"

Kallie took a deep breath and steeled herself for the conversation she had been trying to plan. *Here goes nothing...*

"I *was* working that night, and it was so crazy. I had to talk to the police and stuff."

"Oh, wow. Weren't you scared?"

"At first, yeah, it was pretty scary," Kallie admitted, truthfully. "I felt like the murderer was following me for a while. I heard you were mixed up in it too. Didn't one of the suspects eat here that night, or something?" *Mess up the details a little so it sounds casual*, she told herself, trying to remain calm and sound unrehearsed.

"Oh, he didn't even really come here," Nicola replied with a wave of her hand. "Harvey lives in the neighborhood and he comes here pretty often, so I knew he wasn't here that night."

"So he lied to the police?"

"Yeah, not too smart, right?" she replied with a sigh. "It's not like we don't have cameras." She gestured at three corners of the room and then leaned over to point down the hallway toward the restrooms. There were security cameras everywhere.

"Wow, did you get robbed or something?"

"No, but since we've become so popular, we have a lot of cash in the register some nights. Especially when we're crowded. My dad thought it was good idea."

"It's definitely a good idea. We have them too."

"Harvey always seemed like a pretty nice guy, to be honest. I don't know him personally, but he's been coming here for years." Nicola fiddled with the salt shaker on the table. "The police and the media have been in here a dozen times in the last few weeks, asking about him."

Nicola seemed like she wanted to talk about her ordeal, which Kallie hadn't anticipated. The whole thing was probably stressing her out too. *I know the feeling, my friend...*

"I saw him on the news, so he's back in town," she tried to reassure her friend. "Hopefully they'll all leave you alone soon."

"I can't wait for it to all be over. I feel awful for that poor girl and her family, but having cops and news trucks in the parking lot is hurting my bottom line. I hope they find her killer soon. and lock him up forever."

"You don't think it's that guy, Harvey Keaton?"

"I mean, it could be. He doesn't seem like the type, but you never know, right? Last winter, one of the kitchen guys said someone took out a restraining order on Keaton."

"A restraining order for what?"

"You work in this industry, Kallie, so you know the restaurant business is all drama and gossip. Some days, I swear there's more scandal than pizza in here. But a few of the guys rent a house from Keaton, and they were saying he beat someone up – I never got the full story whether it was his girlfriend, or a guy who was after his girlfriend... To be honest, I figured they were just mad about a rent increase and wanted to stir the pot. But who knows?"

"Does he seem like the violent type?"

"Not at all. He's always been polite, and he's a good tipper. I don't usually listen to the kitchen gossip, but I wondered about it, because we always have so many young girls waiting tables here." She fidgeted with the salt shaker some more, unscrewing the cap nervously. "And I remember that his hands did look busted up. I even asked him about it, and he said he was repairing the bathroom sink in one of his rental houses."

"When my dad replaced the kitchen faucet, he ripped up his knuckles pretty badly," Kallie agreed, thinking about Nicola's story. *Don't make excuses for violent men, Kalliope.* "But that doesn't mean it's true."

"Yeah. I never saw him in here with a woman, and I never saw him fight with anyone, so I really didn't think of it again until you asked, just now. But it worried me a little at the time, and now that we know he lied to police, it does seem suspicious."

"Did you tell the police?"

"I didn't think of it," Nicola admitted. "But if he

did have a restraining order, the police would know about it, right?"

"Maybe not, if it was issued here in Sarasota."

Nicola pulled a notepad and pen out of her apron pocket, followed by a few folded-up takeout menus, and then recovered a business card. Holding it up, she told Kallie, "One of the detectives gave me his card. I'll call him after the lunch rush is over. Just in case."

The booths were filling up around them, and waitresses were starting to rush around the room, so Kallie could see that Nicola needed to get back to work.

They stood up from their seats and hugged goodbye as Nicola forced a to-go container of Kallie's favorite manicotti into her hands.

"Don't be a stranger, and give my love to your dad!"

As Kallie began the long drive back to Owhiro, though, all she could imagine were those bruised knuckles swinging at Alexandra's face.

* * * * *

Tess was as good as her word, like always. When Kallie went to her house the next day, the back seat of her car was already neatly stitched up with heavy-duty thread, and the biggest gash was covered with an iron-on patch. Her best friend had found an old Adventureland patch that looked like it had been created in about 1976, with the Jungle Cruise and Tiki Room birds embroidered on it.

Kallie loved it. The car didn't look new, but it wasn't. It looked loved and colorful and whole again, and she hugged Tess within an inch of her life.

"Just be sure to watch out for the hippo's wiggling ears, Kal! Do you remember how we hated the Tiki Room until we were about fifteen, and then we thought it was so cool?!" Tess reminded her.

As a Florida native, Kallie had been going to Disneyworld practically since birth, but Tess hadn't moved to the area until fifth grade. Her surprising likes and utter pre-teen disdain had changed the way Kallie looked at everything. "And I'd have that song stuck in my head for days, every time we went there."

Tess whistled a little of the song and laughed. "I knew that would cheer you up a little. Mike's coming over when he wakes up, since he's still on the night shift. I texted him a picture of the outside damage, and he thinks he can fix it cosmetically in an hour. He said it really needs to be welded, but he thinks the technical college in Clearwater can do it for next to nothing, when you're ready."

"You guys are going to make me cry."

"Not again!" Tess teased, hugging her.

"Can we drop off the Banana Barge now?"

"What, you don't want to keep it for another few days? We could swing by your ex's house in it!"

"Don't even joke," Kallie laughed. "He'd probably offer to buy it from me!"

"Let's keep it one more night, just in case Mike has any problems with your door. I'll drive you to the rental place after he gets a look at the damage."

"Deal."

Chapter Fourteen

The next day, after they came back from dropping off the annoying but now-hilarious Banana Barge at the car rental office, Kallie mentioned the call with her mother.

"Ugh! You're helping your mom track down your brother? *Why?!*" Tess asked.

"Mostly so she'll stop calling me," Kallie answered with an eye roll. "She seems like she's actually worried, though, which surprises me."

"I'm sure Jack's fine, apart from his usual dysfunction – and hopefully keeping his trouble *far* from here."

"No kidding. I'd like to keep at least five hundred miles between us."

"Remember that time he chased you out of your parents' house on Christmas day, when we were sixteen? And we ended up at the Chinese restaurant because it was the only place open?"

"And we didn't have any money, and that nice older couple bought us shrimp fried rice for dinner and listened to us cry."

"He's such a slimeball," Tess mumbled.

"I still go to that restaurant whenever I'm up in Gulfport, you know," Kallie admitted. "I'm glad you were with me."

"Me too. Thank goodness for the kindness of strangers," Tess replied, accenting the last few words like Blanche DuBois.

"I don't want Jack anywhere near me, but I worry about his stupid drug habit."

"They both act like he's dealing with some dangerous international drug cartel. Isn't he using some kind of ADHD medicine? I don't think he's going to get stuffed into a sixty-five-gallon drum over Ritalin."

"Maybe I should have *you* talk to our mother," Kallie responded with a laugh. "Anyway, I'm sure he won't call me, but if he doesn't call my mother soon, I'll see if I can find some of his useless friends. Those moochers never let him get too far away."

* * * * *

"Well, if the fiancé isn't the murderer – and he does seem to have a pretty airtight alibi – then it has to be the landlord." Kallie announced later, out of the blue, still thinking about her conversation with Nicola. She hadn't mentioned the Sarasota side-trip to Tess yet.

"Are we starting this again?" Tess groaned.

"I'm not going to stake out the landlord's rental

house for five hours, like we did with Jimmy Davis, if that's what you mean."

"You were *sure* it was the fiancé, remember?"

"You were pretty sure, too, as I recall."

"But it *wasn't*," Tess reminded her. "You can't keep stalking everyone Lex knew. Let the cops do their jobs."

"The St Pete police don't have time to worry about one little murder in Owhiro. They have bigger problems to handle in their own city."

"This is a major murder. I'm sure they're still investigating it."

"You're just saying that now because you have a crush on Detective Morrison," Kallie replied with a smirk. "When's the last time you saw it mentioned on the news?"

"About a week ago," Tess admitted. "But that doesn't mean they aren't working on it. They just stopped having press conferences about it."

Nicola's story about Keaton was still giving Kallie the creeps, though. If she told Tess the story, her friend would definitely say she was crazy, so she kept it to herself – along with her increasing commitment to help the poor murdered girl.

"I just want to check out the landlord. I promise not to get involved."

"Check him out? What does that even mean?"

Tess asked. "You can't afford a private detective, and the police won't give you any information about him."

"I haven't decided yet. I'll think about it after work."

* * * * *

After another series of nightmares, though – where a shadowy man chased her through the Lazy Gecko with a meat cleaver – her decision was pretty simple. On Sunday, her next day off, Kallie made the drive to Sarasota again, with another destination in mind.

After looking up Alexandra's rental house for directions, she parked a block away and walked down the sidewalk, wondering how much she'd be able to investigate. As she approached, though, she was surprised to see Keaton himself in front of the house. She pretended to be texting with someone as she walked, heart racing, until the landlord finished locking the door.

Yikes, I need a story, quick.

"Excuse me," Kallie stopped him, wishing she could snarl at him, but hoping to charm him with a big smile instead. "I'm sorry to bother you, but my husband and I are moving into this area, and we're looking for a place to live. Someone in town told me this house was available."

"Oh," the landlord stumbled for a moment. "I... yes, ma'am, it will be available soon. The old tenant just... left. Recently."

Kallie fought the urge to say something nasty. *How shady could this guy be?*

"We're catching our flight home to Minneapolis tonight. Is there any chance I could look at the house today? I understand it wouldn't be in perfect condition—" she insisted before he could argue. "I could just take a few photos of the inside, to show my husband, and then I'll be out of your way."

"I'm not sure—"

"We love this neighborhood so much," Kallie cooed, "and everything we've seen here has been *right* in our price range."

Dollar signs lit up in his eyes. *Creep.*

"I suppose it wouldn't hurt," Keaton replied. "You understand that I haven't had time to hire anyone to clean up yet. The last tenant left very suddenly, so her belongings are still here."

"Of course, of course. I'm an interior decorator," Kallie stretched her creative lying a little more, "so I'll be able to picture the house with our own furniture."

The landlord turned and started walking back up the pathway to the front door of the cute little cottage. Kallie followed slowly, looking for any sign of disturbance or— What exactly *was* she looking for? She hoped she'd know if she saw it.

* * * * *

The tiny house was immaculate, with a beautiful canal view from the back patio. It was half the size of her own home, but Kallie knew the rent must be at least five times her monthly mortgage payment.

The landlord showed her around each of the small rooms, and Kallie was smitten with the gorgeous, colorful furnishings and black and white photos on the living room walls. The kitchen was small but elegant, with high-end appliances and large windows, which opened directly onto the patio over the water. She photographed it all.

"So the previous tenant just abandoned the place?" she asked, pretending to be oblivious.

"I'm afraid so," he replied. "She wasn't even late on the rent, she seems to have just vanished. You know how flighty these young women today can be."

Or maybe you killed her, Kallie thought to herself. He must not have committed the crime here, though, or it would've been more convenient to just dump her body in the canal.

He still seems like the most likely culprit, though. Kallie thought of Nicola's story about Keaton again and suddenly wondered about the wisdom in meeting him here alone. Glancing into her purse at her can of pepper spray, she reminded herself that she needed to be the voice for Lex, since she could no longer defend herself.

"So does the furniture come with the rental?" she asked with a cheerful smile, taking a few more pictures with her phone, for her make-believe husband. She couldn't even afford a single month's rent on her bartending tips, but Keaton didn't need to know that. "Some of these pieces are quite lovely." She stroked the velvet of a graceful wingback chair that must have been a hundred years old. The furniture pieces didn't match, but instead complemented each other perfectly — and that was Kallie's decorating style too.

"I believe there's a ninety-day waiting period on that," Keaton replied. "I'll need to check with the county. But if she doesn't claim them, I'm sure we could work something out."

The hallway was filled with a row of ten miniature, hand-painted landscapes and still life artwork. The tiny details were amazing, and Kallie also suspected they were antiques. By contrast, the small bedroom was brightly lit by large windows, and a huge painting of local Florida birds in flight covered one entire wall.

Whoever Alexandra Clemons was, Kallie thought to herself, *I wish I'd known her. This place feels like the home of my soul sister.*

If the police were going to back-burner this case, Kallie felt even more compelled to help in some way. She hadn't expected to find a huge pool of dried blood or anything, but she was disappointed that her amateur sleuthing hadn't turned up any useful clues inside the house.

Walking out onto the wooden patio, Keaton remarked that it was his favorite place in the house. Kallie had to agree that the view was breathtaking.

"My husband would love this patio. He grills outside on ours, but it's small and the lake attracts mosquitos."

"They aren't a problem out here because of the breeze from the canal."

"And there's plenty of room out here," she went on — trying to make conversation while she subtly checked for evidence, taking photos on her phone throughout. It really was beautiful, though.

"There are a few other people interested," the landlord hinted.

I'll bet, she thought.

Chapter Fifteen

"You did *what*?!" Tess yelled.

"But I mean, the house isn't off limits. The landlord is trying to rent it out again, so people are going to be walking through there every day."

"I know, but—"

"And he said there are other people interested already, so I didn't have time to wait."

"Kallie, you went there *alone*?"

"I had my pepper spray," Kallie replied sheepishly, holding it up for Tess like that explained everything. "And I had a good story about my husband—"

Tess sighed loudly. "Look, don't do it again. No matter what. Any more of these crazy missions – I'm going *with* you from now on. Agreed?"

Kallie nodded silently, still feeling guilty and a little foolish.

"So what did you find?"

"Not much," Kallie sighed in return. "I didn't see any blood or any sign of a struggle. So maybe Hannah's right, and the knocked-over stuff was just a coincidence. I took a bunch of pictures, though."

She handed her phone to Tess, who sat down and started scanning through Kallie's new pictures from the rental house.

"It really feels like nobody else is trying to find Lex's killer anymore, Tess," she said with a sad expression. "It's just me."

"Hey," Tess interrupted. "And me."

Kallie hugged her best friend around the shoulders as she kept looking through the pictures. "And you," she agreed.

Kallie's dad joined them a few minutes later, tired of tinkering in the garage. He sat next to Tess and looked over her shoulder at the phone. "Cute house. Are these pictures of Alexandra's rental?"

Tess nodded and started to explain, but he stopped her with a resigned chuckle. "Don't tell me, I don't want to know. Plausible deniability."

"What's this on the patio?" Tess asked, pointing at one of the pictures, blown up on Kallie's phone.

"I think Lex was grilling out there. Probably vegetables or fish," Kallie answered, remembering that Alexandra was a healthy eater. "It was just a burn mark and some spilled barbeque sauce, not blood."

"Seriously?" Tess asked, surprised.

"I scratched it to check, when he wasn't looking. Definitely barbeque sauce."

"Dang, girl," Tess laughed.

"Well, you did call me Miss Poirot," Kallie replied, striking a theatrical pose. "I gotta keep up my image."

"What's this in the kitchen?" her dad asked a few minutes later, squinting at the phone and reaching for his glasses.

Kallie took the phone back from Tess so she could look more closely.

"The paper on the fridge," he added.

"I didn't even notice that when I was taking the picture," Kallie answered, expanding the photo. Squinting at it herself, she saw a single handwritten note pinned to the refrigerator with a magnet. "It says 'C&W Trust.' I wonder what that is? It sounds like some kind of bank, maybe?"

Tess pulled out her own phone and searched in the browser for a minute. "I don't see anything online about a bank with that name. But her family had tons of money, so maybe it's some kind of trust fund in an offshore account in the Cayman Islands or something."

Kallie nodded, handing her phone back to Tess so she could finish looking at the photos.

"You know, Keaton might really be dangerous, and if he lied to the cops about his alibi then he's reckless too." Tess looked up from the phone. "I'll admit, it's been fun digging through all of these possible clues, but maybe the police need to be the ones looking into this guy."

"The police are still looking at *Mike*," Kallie replied grumpily.

"They need to follow the evidence, even if it means looking at Mike, Kallie. Even if it seems like they're taking a long time. And listen, if the police have to use you as a witness in the trial, you can't be biased by all this research."

Kallie's forehead crinkled at the change in subject. "What?"

"Detective Morrison explained it to me when we were at the station. It's not that he doesn't want your input. He just wants to make sure they get the guy and lock him up for good. That's all."

"I can't be a witness, though. I didn't see anything. I was in the bar all night, remember?"

"Don't ask me. That's just what he said. There are different kinds of witnesses, so he must have something in mind."

"I guess..."

"And I'm sure he doesn't want you to get hurt. The murderer might be watching the police, and maybe even watching you too – and you haven't exactly been subtle."

"*WHAT*? I've been *totally* subtle."

Tess rolled her eyes dramatically and sighed.

159

"Just think about it, okay? And don't go on any other wild goose chases without me."

* * * * *

Kallie pulled the ornate brass tap for one of the local microbrewery beers, pouring two pints while chatting to Teddy. "I tried the soup on Wednesday after I fished my shift, and it was as good as you said. I even brought some home for my dad."

"It's much better with air conditioning," he replied, seeming tired and inattentive.

"No kidding. I don't know how we survived for two days in the hottest time of the year. Thanks for sticking it out with me and finding the repairman."

"Wouldn't you rather have gone home?"

"Well, I couldn't have gone home. I had to finish my shift. But I *would* have preferred to go hide in the walk-in freezer all day."

She carried the two beers over to a pair of elderly men who were playing dominoes in one of the booths. She hadn't seen them before, but they were apparently regulars on this shift. Kallie had never worked on a Sunday afternoon before, and it was another completely different atmosphere.

The Lazy Gecko wasn't a sports bar, but they turned the digital displays over to the Rays baseball games on Sunday afternoons in the two main rooms. It was noisy and distracting, and drew a bigger, louder crowd.

As she returned to the bar, Cici arrived and slumped onto the stool next to Teddy. Her two favorite patrons didn't usually come in on weekends, but today they rolled in early, looking a little worse for wear. Teddy looked exhausted, and even Cecelia's colorful clothes and carefully styled hair couldn't hide the bags under her eyes.

"Two Bloody Marys please, Kallie. Make mine a double. No celery." Teddy couldn't even force a smile.

"Long night?" Kallie asked, looking a little worried.

"My brother's in town," Cici answered. "He's a bit of a partier. Could you make mine with rum, please? I don't think I can stomach vodka today."

"That bad, huh?" Kallie asked with a sympathetic smile. "You got it."

"Oh, no Worcestershire in mine, either," she added when she saw the bottle.

"She's a vegetarian," Teddy chimed in.

"Oh, that's very healthy."

"I'm not a *healthy* vegetarian," Cici replied with a wink. "I like my junk food and booze too much. Do you have any hot sauce back there somewhere?"

"Of course! This is a civilized bar. I have Tabasco

or Cholula hot sauce," Kallie offered. "They have Texas Pete back in the kitchen."

"Ooh, Cholula please."

"Cici's brother was a cruise director for ten years, and now he flips houses," Teddy grunted. "His liver's made of lead."

"I tried telling him we're too old for that stuff—"

"But then he breaks out the añejo, and—"

"We can't seem to say no," they completed the thought in unison and laughed tiredly.

"No worries, your 'hair of the dog' is on the way, my dears. Dill pickle?"

"Yes, please!" Cici chirped.

"Where's your brother now? He didn't come with you?" Kallie asked, tucking a pickle spear into her Cubanita and handing it over. "Is he still asleep?"

"Ha! He was up at the crack of dawn to go for a five-mile run."

"He's a cyborg," her husband grimaced, sipping his drink. "Hopefully he's out puking in the mangroves somewhere. He hadn't come back by the time we left."

"I left him a note that we'd be back by four p.m."

The revitalizing drink began working its hangover-reducing magic, and Teddy turned to watch the baseball game.

Kallie grabbed two menus from a passing server, guessing they'd want food too. They both still looked pretty miserable.

"They don't serve breakfast, do they?" Cici asked.

"Closest thing he makes is a burger with a fried egg on top."

Cici turned a bit green. "Gross."

Kallie laughed in agreement. It sounded disgusting to her too, but it was one of their biggest sellers.

"I'll have the veggie quesadillas. Teddy, do you want something from the kitchen?"

"Soup?" he asked, not looking away from the game.

"It's chili on Sundays."

"Sounds good."

"He's such a talker," Cici smirked. "You can never get him to shut up."

"But he's so agreeable." Kallie replied with a laugh.

Cici smiled at that, nodding, and slid over to watch the game with him.

* * * * *

"Hang on, let's watch this," Kallie called to Tess when they met at home later. Kallie was fixing dinner and Tess was working on the abandoned jigsaw puzzle. "It's more about the murder."

"There hasn't been anything new lately," Tess answered, grabbing the remote control and turning up the volume on the local news. "And I don't want to watch her dad again."

"Yeah, me neither. Poor guy. Who's this lady?"

A male reporter was interviewing another young woman, not as pretty as Lex, and she looked very studious, with glasses and a severe haircut. The label on the screen said she was Lex's business partner.

"I haven't heard anything about a business. She must be involved with the charity."

"Penny Jameson," Tess mused, reading from the updated box at bottom of the tv screen. "I don't remember Lex's dad or the fiancé mentioning her."

"Morrison never mentioned her either," Kallie grumbled, turning the stove down so she could leave the kitchen. She sat down in the living room, where she could hear the interview better.

"People are wondering why you didn't report Alexandra missing in those first few days, when she remained unidentified," the reporter addressed the young woman. "Can you explain that?"

"I've told the police everything I know,"

Jameson answered the reporter, who seemed to have caught her by surprise outside her house. "I hadn't seen Lex at the office in a few days, because she was out scouting for neighborhoods that could use our help. That's how she was. Always looking for someone to help," she added, with a choked sob.

"Can this get any worse? It seems like everyone adored her, and she was trying to help even *more* kids?" Kallie groaned.

"Please, someone must know something," Penny was still talking, and she addressed the camera directly. "Lex was such a kind, generous person, and she didn't deserve this. There's a big reward for information. Please just talk to the police." She turned away from the reporter, obviously uncomfortable with crying on camera.

The reporter gave the phone number for the local crime tip line, and the station cut back to older footage of the victim's heartbroken father. His misery was apparently great for ratings, but Kallie couldn't bear it. She muted the television.

"Even if I wasn't accidentally involved, how can we not try to help solve this? I mean, no one deserves to be murdered, but it sounds like Lex was a really nice kid."

"What did she say about opening a new building?" Tess asked.

"Who? The business partner? I didn't hear that

part. Rewind it."

"It was when you were in the kitchen. I think she said it was part of the charity's plan to work with the local kids."

Tess rewound the news segment until Penny Jameson was back on the screen.

"Shush this time," she teased Kallie as the story restarted.

"Lex's big dream was to open an arts center for disadvantaged kids," her business partner said. "I was doing a lot of research on available properties online, but she was doing the legwork. She'd been driving out to look at different locations all over Tampa Bay."

"To find land for an arts center?" the reporter asked. "Couldn't she just put it anywhere?"

"She wanted a place that was away from the city, with enough space for a musical studies building, and a separate visual arts center. She wanted to add a theater building one day, too. And lots of land, just so it would be a peaceful, safe, beautiful place for under-served kids to hang out. She was even going to have a shuttle bus to pick up the kids after school."

The cameraman cut back to the reporter for his response, but he just looked stunned.

"She wanted to open a place near here, in Sarasota, but couldn't find enough available land."

"That sounds pretty amazing," the reporter

replied, and then his face fell as he seemed to realize that it wasn't going to happen anymore. "Did she ever find anything?"

"She did. She found two adjacent lots that she wanted to buy and was trying to convince the owners to sell. Once I was able to get into her computer a few days ago, I found out that she had even started the paperwork on her offer."

The reporter didn't reply, but Kallie's instinct assured her that this was related to the murder.

"We're going to continue with a new center in Pasco County, if we can complete the land purchase. It's in a little town called Devotion, which her notes said 'sounded just perfect.' It probably won't be all that she imagined, of course, but it's what Lex would have wanted."

The reporter recovered his senses and began asking, "People are wondering why you didn't report—"

Tess muted the tv again as the segment reached the place where they'd begun watching.

"Wow, a huge new arts center for underprivileged kids. That actually doesn't surprise me at all," Kallie reflected. "And she had great taste, so I bet it would've been amazing."

"I'm sure we can find something online about

the center if the planning and development were already underway," Tess replied. "There would have been legal papers filed and licenses requested, and maybe some architectural designs. Maybe even a purchase offer, if she got that far. And there are probably some 'community feature' stories in the local news, too."

"Wait, so you're still in this with me?"

"You say that like you're surprised."

Chapter Sixteen

Tess sent an email from her office the next day, where she was apparently bored while her boss was on vacation. "I found an old article online, from the Sarasota newspaper's website. It's a year old, so it's not about the new center, but it's about Lex and her charity."

Kallie clicked the link in the email when she got home from work, popping up an article on the Sarasota Herald-Tribune website titled 'DC Transplant Saves After-School Center.' The article said Alexandra Clemons 'chipped in' to save a local rec center that was in danger of closing.

That must have been one huge chip, Kallie thought to herself. She remembered when that story was on the news last year, and the rec center needed a *lot* of money. Their building needed a lot of repairs, due to degradation and mold where the rain was coming in, and the landlord abandoned the place instead of fixing the damage. They were looking for donations to stay afloat, but they really needed someone to buy the place and fix it up.

There would be zero return on investment, she remembered. They were basically looking for a guardian angel. Someone to save the place out of the goodness of their heart, simply because the closure would leave a whole bunch of little kids with nowhere safe to go after school.

And they'd found their angel in Lex.

She sent an email back: "So when are we going to Pasco County?"

* * * * *

"I think you're getting addicted to this whole 'creepy murder suspect hunting' thing, Kal."

"Well, my brother's addicted to stupid schoolkid drugs, and my mother's addicted to... herself," Kallie replied. "There are worse things."

Tess blinked at her silently, visibly biting her tongue.

"Okay, maybe this addiction is a little more dangerous than some," Kallie corrected herself, catching her best friend's frustrated expression. "But at least it doesn't hurt anyone."

Blink. Blink.

"Okay, maybe it could hurt me. If I end up chasing someone dangerous. But no one else."

Squint.

Kallie sighed. "Okay, you too. And my dad and

Sherman. But this is important."

"I know it's important. But you could leave it up to the *police*, like Detective Morrison keeps saying."

"He's not even looking at anything anymore. He's still so convinced that it's Mike, he won't even listen to reason."

"He won't listen to the random babbling of a traumatized bartender who's been reading too much Agatha Christie and has no idea what she's talking about? *Shocking!*" Tess snapped.

Kallie laughed, embarrassed, as she walked to the kitchen to get another two slices of Mrs. Cooper's pound cake. "I know you're right, but this is personal now."

"I know it is. I worried about the nightmares and panic attacks you were having, even after you stopped telling me about them," Tess replied with another annoyed squint. "Yes, I could tell. I'm not blind."

Kallie blushed and picked at her fingernails.

"But the more I hear about this girl, the more I want to help too. But we need to do it *safely*, Kal. Research, not confrontation. And we'll let the police handle the dangerous part, right?"

"Fine," Kallie sighed.

Tess took a bite of the pound cake and nodded agreeably. "This cake is amazing. Are you sure your dad doesn't like this lady? She might be a keeper."

"She's as creepy as the rest, but she's definitely a better cook." Between bites, Kallie asked, "Just this one last stakeout, okay? If I'm wrong, then I promise I'll leave it up to Morrison."

"I can't believe you just called it a stakeout," Tess answered with a laugh, shaking her head. "Fine. One last check on the plot of land at the courthouse in Pasco County. That seems harmless."

* * * * *

"Okay, so explain to me what we're looking for this time?" Tess asked as she drove north to find more information on Alexandra's mysterious planned investment.

"Buying land is pretty stressful, right?" Kallie paused at looked at her best friend, who knew this was true from recent first-hand experience.

"Buying and selling, both," Tess agreed, reflecting on the annoying, cut-throat sellers of her own home. "It's a nightmare. But only for a little while. And it's not worth killing over."

"Nothing's worth killing over, but it happens every day."

"Sure, kids get killed over tennis shoes, but that's not what happened here. The cops would have solved it in fifteen minutes."

"I just have a feeling about this. A young, rich woman, out alone in a fancy car, in a rural area with no witnesses, maybe offering a lot of money to some strange guy who saw an easy victim?"

"I think you're daydreaming, Kal."

"Probably, but it's my day off, and you said you'd help."

"Honey, just because I think you're bonkers doesn't mean I'm backing out of your crazy plan," Tess laughed, grabbing Kallie's hand encouragingly. "We haven't had this much adventure in years. Besides, I like crime dramas, even if they're idiotic."

Kallie laughed out loud, crossing her eyes and sticking her tongue out at Tess, and then cranked up the radio as they sped along the northbound freeway.

* * * * *

Kallie and Tess didn't get very far with their research at the Pasco County courthouse, but a word of advice from that office led them to the nearby Recorder of Deeds office. There, they quickly learned that they could have looked up the documents online.

The polite and helpful assistant at the front desk took their information, though, commenting that they rarely had in-person visitors anymore, and she was happy to help.

After explaining their research request at the front desk, they found that there was nothing available about the rec center in Sarasota – which they expected, since they were in the wrong county – and the new deeds hadn't been signed yet because Lex hadn't convinced the owners to sell. So there was nothing on file. It looked like a dead end after all.

As they started to leave, the assistant called them back. "Did you say the land was in Devotion?"

"Yes, do you know where that is?"

"My grandmother lives near there, in Zephyrhills. Devotion is a tiny town, like blink-and-you'll-miss-it tiny. I'll bet there aren't more than a half a dozen large parcels of land. That's public record, so if you think it was over five acres, I can bring you what we have."

"Thank you so much," Kallie gushed, surprised at the offer.

"It's no problem, and it'll give me something to do. Like I said, we don't get very many visitors now that everything's online."

Fifteen minutes later, she returned with eight manila folders, explaining that it was a few more than she expected. There was a reading room where they could sit and examine them, she added, pointing the way.

Soon squeezed side by side at a huge mahogany table with old fashioned reading lamps, Kallie and Tess started reading the long, complicated documents together. All of the land parcels were large and full of mature trees – and a few had water frontage listed, which they thought must be creeks. But only two of the eight lots were side-by-side.

"Penny Jameson said she was interested in buying two adjacent lots in the Devotion area. It must be these two," Kallie spoke quietly, as if they were in a library. She slid the other folders down the table, so they could focus on the most likely pair.

Tess opened the folders and slid the two property survey drawings together, to show the combined land. "Both of these lots have houses on them. If she was going to knock them down, that could make some enemies," she suggested.

"Look at these property values, though," Kallie pointed out. "These houses are in the middle of nowhere, and the houses look pretty crappy from the photos. I'll bet she was offering more than they're worth."

"From what we've heard about her, that's probably a pretty good guess."

"I think she was just trying to do the right thing. The houses are on big, rural lots, perfect for a safe, fun retreat for disadvantaged kids. If she was going to tear someone's house down, she seems like the kind of girl who would pay them well for their trouble."

"What a freak," Tess joked sarcastically, halfheartedly, and then sighed.

"Yeah, she seemed like a class act. We really need to figure this out, Tess."

"We will."

Kallie paged through the first of the deeds, to the very last page, and found something that surprised her.

"Whoa."

Tess looked up from the other folder. "What?"

Kallie silently pointed at the back page, where the deed was signed by the current owners. The signatures were illegible, but the name typed underneath was as clear as a spring day.

"C&W Trust," Tess read out loud. "That was the name on Lex's refrigerator. I guess it's not a bank, after all."

"I think we're finally on the right track here."

Kallie wrote down the addresses of the two lots, and flipped through the grainy, copied photographs again – taking duplicate pictures on her phone. Then they returned all of the files to the front desk, with repeated thanks to their bored and helpful assistant.

"So as long as we're all the way up in Dade City, we might as well keep going to Devotion, right?"

"Might as well."

* * * * *

"Stop tapping your foot," Tess whispered. "You're making me nervous."

"Sorry," Kallie whispered back. She pulled her foot up into the passenger seat and sat on it, knowing she wouldn't be able to stop. *What if I'm wrong about all of this? Tess will think I'm crazy. What if I'm right, and the murderer kills us both?* She started biting her thumb nail instead.

"Are you sure this is the right house?" Tess whispered.

"This is the one on the first deed for the arts center. I wrote down the addresses."

Tess nodded, then sat quietly for a while.

The assistant at the Deeds office hadn't been kidding, Devotion was tiny town. There wasn't even a town center, with stores or a supermarket, it was what Kallie's dad would have called "a wide place in the road" – just a few houses in close proximity. She suspected one family had owned all this land, at one time, and chose the town name.

"So we're just going to sit here?" Tess finally asked.

"Yep, I just want to see who lives here first."

"Because you'll be able to tell if the owner is a murderer, when you see them?" Tess asked, with a raised eyebrow.

"I'm hoping for a sign. A bright, glaring, neon sign."

"*Okayyyy—*"

"Maybe the owner will be a frail ninety-year-old woman?" *Hopefully,* she added to herself.

"Do you think that's likely?"

"I guess we'll find out."

* * * * *

After half an hour of watching a bunch of nothing, and trying not to fidget, Kallie's ability to sit still was failing.

"I'm just going to walk around the property a little," she decided.

"Are you sure that's a good idea, Kal? We're in the middle of nowhere out here."

"I'll shuffle my feet to scare off the snakes. I promise not to get in any trouble – I just have a feeling about this place."

"Okay," Tess relented. "I'm staying here to keep an eye on the door of the house, and I'll honk if I see anything, uh..."

"Scary?"

"Scary, dangerous, creepy, ugly. Anything

moving at all, probably."

Kallie hugged her best friend on the spur of the moment, and took a quick look around before stepping out of the car.

"I'll just be a few minutes."

Tess folded her arms tightly across her chest and nodded, looking small in the driver's seat and obviously wishing they were somewhere else. Kallie shut the car door quietly and started walking back toward the street and around the perimeter of the poorly maintained old house. There were two houses on Alexandra's list, but she had a gut suspicion about this one.

Kallie didn't want to be arrested for trespassing, so she stuck to the outside edge of the long driveway and side street – peering into the shady spaces under the trees and around the many dilapidated appliances and rusty vehicles in the dead grass.

A few times she glimpsed movement, and turned to watch, heart skipping a beat – but the rustling was almost always caused by the light breeze, which was doing nothing to alleviate the heat.

Once it was a mama raccoon trundling out of an overturned wheelbarrow with a few babies. Looking for more shade, probably, near the front porch. Kallie stood on the edge of the street – having circled all the way around the front yard, and brushed her hair off her sweaty forehead, watching the fat babies navigate the brown weeds, momentarily. She wished she'd brought a bottle of water.

"*What are you doing in my yard?*" a voice snarled behind her.

The voice was so close that Kallie could feel his breath on her neck. She hadn't even heard him coming. She whipped around and a saw a towering, scrawny man with wild yellow hair, so close she could smell him.

"I said," he began again, voice suddenly rising in heart-stopping, mindless anger, "*WHAT ARE YOU DOING IN MY YARD?!*"

He was suddenly inches away from Kallie, in her face, spittle hitting her eyelids as she tried to back away blindly. She stumbled over an old tree stump and fought to stay on her feet, knowing that he would attack her if she hit the ground.

"I'm looking for my cat," she whimpered, forcing out the only lie that sprang to her terrified mind. *I thought I wanted to find the killer, and now he found me, instead.* "I lost my cat, and I thought I saw him in your yard."

"You're not looking for your cat," he hissed in her ear, leaning so close that she could see the beads of sweat on his neck. He suddenly yelled, straight in her ear, "*I SAW YOU HERE, WATCHING ME.*"

He lunged toward her, and she finally fell over the old stump's roots, landing on her backside in the sand and weeds.

180

"My cat, I swear I'm just looking for my cat. He's orange." She was so terrified of this psychotic, screaming man, she didn't even know what else to say. She turned her face away and closed her eyes, whining back over her shoulder, "Orange and white. Orange with a blue collar."

A white truck passed in the street, screeching its tires and honking at something, and distracted the crazy man for a moment. Kallie took her only chance. She scrambled toward the asphalt, tearing up her hands in the process, hoping she'd be safer in the open street. *Will he chase me? Would anyone in this neighborhood even care?*

Once her feet hit the pavement and found traction, away from the slippery weeds and sand, she ran as fast as she could. One glance back, and she saw his right arm in the air — thinking he might have a gun — but he only threw his half-empty beer bottle after her.

"AND STAY AWAY! DON'T LET ME CATCH YOU HERE AGAIN!" he screamed at her, turning back toward the house.

"Not without Morrison, you won't," she swore out loud to herself, tears in her eyes, hands still shaking.

181

Chapter Seventeen

"That freak could have killed you, Kallie. You need to stop this now," Tess insisted. She'd whipped out of the side street at warp speed when Kallie jumped back in the car, and they were now stopped in a parking lot. Back in civilization.

"How can I stop? We're so close. He's probably the killer, we just need to figure out why."

"You don't know he's the killer, honey. You just know he's totally unhinged. And if he kills *you*, it's not going to help you get justice for Lex."

"Tess, I need to do this," Kallie protested. "Can't you understand?"

"I understand that you're obsessed. And I understand that you're trying to do the right thing. But can you at least think of me? And your dad? Consider your own safety, for our sake? What's your dad going to do if you end up dead?"

"Eat a lot more German chocolate cake?"

"It's not funny, Kallie!" Tess snapped.

"It's a little funny," she mumbled. "Fine, I'll take Morrison with me. And ask him to bring backup."

"I guess that's the best I'm going to get. You could let Morrison *go alone.*"

"I'm in too deep now. The whole thing is too overwhelming, and I think about it all the time. If I try to stay home, I'll just drive myself crazy."

"I think that ship has sailed, honey."

Kallie finally smiled at that. "True."

* * * * *

"Sorry, Miss Brooks," Morrison apologized, returning to the phone after another interruption in his office. "Tell me again, you think the Owhiro murder has something to do with the victim's charity organization?"

"They were trying to buy a piece of land up in Pasco County. Alexandra wanted to build an arts center for kids. Painting and stuff, but musical instruments and pottery and writing classes too."

"I saw that. Wasn't she from Sarasota, though?"

"Yeah, but you know, there's no land available down there. It's all being built up with condos and hotels. She found a place north of the Bay and was trying to buy a couple of houses so she could use the land, but she had some kind of problem." She conveniently left out the part about the screaming lunatic homeowner, for the moment.

"What kind of problem?"

"That's why I'm talking to you," she answered with an audible smile. "I haven't been able to figure that part out. She had plenty of money—"

"So the owner didn't want to sell?"

Kallie didn't answer.

"You don't know."

"I don't know," she confirmed. "We could only find the existing deeds that were on file with the county. No details about the pending contract or the owners, but we know the purchase didn't go through before she was killed."

"And you're telling me this because—?"

"Can't you go up there and check? Interview the homeowners, at least?" she huffed.

"Miss Brooks, I don't have any jurisdiction in Pasco County."

"Oh."

"Do you even know what city it was in? I can't ask the Pasco County sheriff's office to investigate, but I know two or three cops up there—"

"Would you do that?" Kallie asked, hopefully.

The detective sighed in barely concealed annoyance. "I know you don't believe this, Miss Brooks, but I want to solve this murder just as much as you do. Maybe more. And *not* just because it's my job."

Kallie had the decency to feel embarrassed for thinking he didn't care about Alexandra Clemons.

"But *some* of us can't go around harassing taxpayers and stalking landlords," he continued. "I'd get our county sued if I did *half* of what you've done."

Kallie noticed that he didn't say it was a bad thing, but she wisely kept her mouth shut. "It's in a little town called Devotion."

"Okay, sure, I've driven past that exit on Highway 56. We have some degree of reciprocity with the other bay area counties, but they're just as understaffed as we are, right now. We're still waiting on quite a bit of paperwork to be sent. I'd appreciate it, if I could look over what you found."

"I'll bring you the information that I got from the county. It has the addresses." Kallie agreed.

"Thanks. I'll see what I can do."

* * * * *

"They finally found Alexandra's Audi," Hannah told Kallie, sipping an iced coffee in the passenger seat of her parked car. They had been texting regularly, and finally met in person again, although they had to make it quick so Kallie could get to work.

"It was dumped down by the everglades," Hannah continued. "Two kids found it, and they got

185

some good pictures and video before they called the cops and claimed the reward. It was full of empty potato chip bags and candy wrappers, plus a ton of cigarette butts."

Kallie tried to nonchalantly kick a candy wrapper under the seat, self-consciously.

Hannah passed her tablet over, and Kallie looked at the photos from Lex's trashed car. "Ooh, Swedish Fish. He has good taste, for a slimy murderer."

"Yeah, all of this stuff must've belonged to someone else. Everyone who knew Lex said she was a health nut. She wasn't the type to eat a lot of candy and junk food. And she definitely wasn't a smoker."

"No way," Kallie agreed. "I was in her house. There was no sign or smell of smoking. Not even outside."

"But they're probably not from the killer, either, unless he was wearing gloves. He was way too careful about not leaving any clues. No fingerprints, nothing. So this stuff probably didn't belong to him – it would be too reckless."

"That makes sense," Kallie nodded. "Well, the police will check every single wrapper, cigarette butt, and scrap of cellophane for evidence, I'm sure. Even though we won't hear about it."

Hannah nodded, and Kallie wondered again who her mysterious contact in the police station was. *Would she hear about the forensic results?*

"Maybe the killer paid someone to dump the car?" Kallie considered.

"Ehhh. That'd be pretty risky with such an expensive, eye-catching car."

"That's true. The driver would've ratted him out if he got pulled over. So maybe he just handed the car keys to some 'lucky' person at random?"

"Or left it running downtown with the doors conveniently unlocked?" Hannah suggested, sipping her coffee and biting the corner off a scone.

"That sounds more likely. Then no one can identify him."

"But then the everglades location would probably just be a coincidence, not a clue about the killer."

"Yeah," Kallie agreed. "The driver probably just ran out of gas on the way to Miami. Or Key West."

"Well, the police will be checking every SunPass monitor and traffic camera for two hundred miles, so I'm sure there will be a photo of the driver on the news by five o'clock," Hannah reassured her. Kallie thought she was leaving, but the blogger added one more thing. "Let me show you something before I go, actually. It might be nothing."

Hannah handed over her tablet again, and Kallie blew up the exposed photo to look closer. "I just got it from one of my sources about an hour ago. I haven't heard anything concrete, and there's no license plate since it's taken from the front – but this looks like her car to me."

"Well, it's definitely an Audi, and that looks like it might be a blonde woman behind the wheel." Kallie squinted, trying to make out the details. "This is a pretty clear shot, even though it was taken after dark. Was she stopped at a business?"

"Yep, exactly."

"When was it taken?"

"The same night she died."

"Oh. Creepy." Kallie replied a little sadly.

"But it's not from her home in Sarasota, and not from Owhiro either. I googled that grocery store in the photo's background, and it's in a shopping center up in Pasco County, out in cow country."

The whole Tampa Bay area was moderately to heavily populated and getting more crowded every year. Kallie knew Pasco County was one of the last places within half an hour of downtown Tampa where you could still buy enough land to keep horses or cows.

"Weird. Her business partner said they were trying to start an arts center up there, and we think we found the place in a town called Devotion. But why would she go up there at night?"

"This picture was taken just outside Odessa." Hannah pulled up a map of the county online. "Yeah, that's at least fifteen miles from Devotion."

"Oh, so maybe it's unrelated to the land she was trying to purchase. I don't really believe in coincidences, but she *could've* just been visiting someone."

"Or maybe she just stopped for coffee on the way back from Devotion?" Hannah suggested, getting out of the car. "I'll let you know if I hear anything else."

* * * * *

Kallie took the finished Fuzzy Pink Blanket of Doom, as she had started to think of it, to Carlos's house the next day before work, wanting to get it to them before the baby was born.

Isabel was still trapped in bed, as ordered by her doctor, and Kallie pulled up a chair so they could talk for a while.

"I brought you my famous marinara sauce and gluten-free noodles, too," she told her friend as she unwrapped the gift. "They're in the fridge. It's supposed to speed up your labor. Now that you're past the danger zone, I figured any old superstition would help."

"That sounds like the best gift ever," Isabel laughed. "I can't wait to get out of this bed."

"I've never seen you sit still for so long!" Kallie, who was fairly athletic and fit, had taken Isabel's aerobics class once, and thought she'd drop dead of exhaustion. She stuck to her yoga classes after that — challenging but not life-threatening.

"Thank goodness for Alicia and Beth! They jumped right in when I had to go on bedrest. I might have lost the studio if it weren't for them." She pulled the garish pink blanket out of its wrapping and snuggled it with a huge smile. "Oh my gosh, thank you. It's so soft! Did you really make it yourself?"

"I did. It took forever," she laughed. "The fluffy yarn did most of the work, and it hides the mistakes."

"Don't say that, you crazy girl! It's beautiful." She leaned forward to hug Kallie, shifting the covers and exposing a tattoo of a stylized dove on her ankle. She caught Kallie looking at it and waved her hand. "It's not real."

"I like it," Kallie told her, sincerely.

"My abuela said a dove symbolizes happy new beginnings. So Carlos drew it on my ankle just to be cute, but I love it," she craned forward and sighed. "He had to take a picture of it with his phone, just to show it to me."

Kallie laughed out loud. "You'll be back to normal any day now."

"I think I'm going to get a permanent tattoo of it, after this girl is hatched and I can see my feet again."

"It's really cool. I didn't know he was an artist."

"Carlos never wants to brag about anything... Well, *you* know how he is." She rolled her eyes with a crooked smile. "But he's really talented. You should get him to take you out to his studio when he gets back. I keep telling him he could sell his work. This is just a little sketch, but his paintings are—"

The front door opened, and their golden retriever started barking joyfully.

"Here he is now. I'll ask him."

"Hey Kallie, are you here?" she heard a call from the front door.

"Hi Carlos!" she yelled back. "I came bearing gifts for your knocked-up, locked-up wife."

Carlos stuck his head in the bedroom door, waving at them. "I saw your car outside. Let me just bring in the groceries."

"He actually likes grocery shopping," Isabel explained after he went back out, "but he spends way too much money. He's always trying to get me new lotions and nail polish and stuff from the cosmetics section."

"Oh, that's weirdly sweet."

"Yeah. And at least they don't make me gag anymore, like they did in my first trimester."

"Are you talking about me?" Carlos asked jokingly as he swung back through the doorway, giving Kallie a big hug. "It's so good to see you. It seems like

191

ages since—"

"Yeah, it does," she cut him off, avoiding the topic, which he seemed to appreciate too. "How's everything going?"

"The same. You know, work is slower now that Spring Break is over, but still crazy. Just the usual craziness. How's the day shift?"

"I expected to hate it, but it's actually pretty cool. A lot less yelling. Hey, did you know we have a kitchen?"

"Where did you think the potato skins came from, Kallie?" he laughed.

"I mean, a real kitchen. People actually come in for the food at lunchtime. Just food. And the tips aren't too bad either."

"Really?"

"Nowhere near as bad as I expected."

"Okay, you two. Enough work talk," Isabel interrupted with a laugh. "Carlos, tell Kallie about your studio."

"Izzy, you told her about—"

"She saw my little dove," she explained, pointing in the general vicinity of her ankle. "Which makes *one* of us."

"I didn't know you could draw!" Kallie admonished him.

"It's just a little sketch—" he protested.

"Your wife already gave you up, Carlos. You're busted. Now take me to see your art studio – if you're ok with that, Isabel?"

"Yes, go. Someone else needs to see his work, so he can't keep it a secret." She hesitated for a second. "But I'd love some of that pasta you brought before you go?"

"Oh my gosh," Kallie jumped up. "I'm starving a pregnant lady! I'm sorry, I should've asked if you were hungry. Let me go fix a bowl right now!"

Carlos followed her out to the kitchen, hoping to help.

"So where is your studio? Is it in Clearwater?" Kallie asked him.

"Oh, no, nothing like that. I just have a little cottage in the backyard. It's small but it has great light." He had obviously given up on trying to change the subject. "I can't believe Izzy told you. But if you really want to see it, I'll grab the keys."

After taking the food to Isabel, they went out the back door, and Kallie saw a small building she had never noticed before. It looked like it had been a mother-in-law suite at one time, but it had been converted into an adorable little studio. Multiple pastel-colored panels intersected with crisp white borders, and it bore a stylish sign labeled 'Studio Alvarez.'

"Wow, Carlos. You could actually have showings out here. This is beautiful."

"That's what Isabel was hoping," he blushed, still uncomfortable with the whole discussion.

"Oh my goodness," Kallie gushed in surprise, as he unlocked the studio door and let her in. "Carlos, these are *beautiful*."

There was a series of six small charcoal portraits next to the door, each about the size of a paperback book. The detail was amazing, even in such a small size. Kallie immediately recognized one of the women as Isabel, but younger.

"These two are my parents, when they were young," he pointed out. "And the rest are my sisters. I have a ton of sisters," he laughed.

"How old is Isabel in this picture?"

"High school," he replied with a smile. "That's when we met. I'm glad you could tell it's her."

"Shut up!" Kallie nudged him in the ribs. "It looks just like her. I could tell she was younger, but it's an incredible likeness."

"I don't usually do portraits, but Izzy really likes those little drawings." He encouraged Kallie to continue into the main room, so he could shut the door.

"Whoa," Kallie exhaled. The rest of the room was filled with a completely different style of artwork. Huge drawings, mostly animals mixed with a few landscapes, all in charcoal or pencil, covered the walls and even the ceiling. A massive, stoic manatee gazed peacefully down at her, next to a Florida panther dozing on a tree limb. A roseate spoonbill was taking flight in tones of grey in the corner, every feather visible. She was stricken silent, staring at the enormous drawings, some of which could almost be mistaken for photographs.

"I like working on this scale," Carlos explained, apparently mistaking her silence for disinterest. "Izzy says it's popular, too, but I don't know who would want to waste a whole wall in their house on my drawings."

"Uh, me?" Kallie immediately answered, turning with a confused expression.

"C'mon, Kallie, I'm being serious."

"So am I!" she insisted. "Can I buy the manatee, before your prices go too high for me to afford it? People will pay buckets of money for these, I promise."

"Oh. Uh, sure. You can just take it, Kal. You're like family."

"I can't just take it. Let me at least pay you for it."

"Okay, give me like thirty bucks. That'll cover the materials. I built the canvas myself, since nobody sells them this size. Be careful, though, it's pretty heavy."

"Thirty bucks? Isabel is going to kill you."

"Is that a no?" he asked, raising an eyebrow.

"Nope." Kallie hurriedly pulled out her wallet and handed him the cash, before he could change his mind. "There's no way it'll fit in my little car, though."

"I'll bring it over to your house after work – if that's not too late for you, these days?"

"It is, but I'll gladly make an exception. And my dad will want to see you, too." She stared at the huge drawing for another minute. "Thank you so much, it's really beautiful. I wish I knew someone who ran an art gallery so I could help you get rich and famous."

"You sound like Izzy," he shook his head. "You two are crazy. Let's get back inside before she misses us too much. I need to try that pasta too."

"It's supposed to get her into labor, so don't eat too much. I brought the finished baby blanket too. You have to see it!"

Chapter Eighteen

"*Hello?!*" Kallie snapped at the caller on her phone, already annoyed. She'd been trying to concentrate on brushing Sherman's fur, which was shedding like crazy in this hot weather, and this was the third time the phone rang. She promised herself that she'd splurge on a call-blocking app for her cell phone tomorrow.

"Hey, Kal. It's me."

She jumped and sat up straight, surprised at a voice she hadn't heard in at least two years. "Jack?!"

"Sure, who else?"

"Mom's looking for you, Jack. I told her to check the county jail. If you're going to ask me to post bail for you, the answer's no."

Kallie's dad, who had been reading on the couch, walked over to the table and sat down silently. He reached out a hand for the phone, and raised an eyebrow, but she waved him off. She wouldn't get him involved unless her brother became verbally abusive.

"Cute. I don't need bail, but I do need help."

"That's rich, you calling me for help. Besides, I've got my own problems right now." *Which of course you couldn't care less about, jerk.*

"This is serious, Kal. I'm in trouble."

Definitely getting that call-blocking app...

She held the phone away from her head, so her dad could hear Jack without putting him on speakerphone. "Call Mom, Jack. You know I don't have any money, especially right now."

"It's not that kind of trouble." Kallie could hear noise in the background, and a man's voice yelling angrily. "I'll call you back," her brother said quickly, and the line went dead.

They both sat in silence for a minute, then her dad said, "Let me talk to him if he calls back."

"He probably just owes money to some skeevy drug dealer, Dad. I don't want you getting involved in that."

"He said it wasn't money."

"Hmm. He did, didn't he?" her forehead wrinkled in thought. "That's weird. Why else would he call me?"

"You're probably the only one who answered the phone. You're too nice for your own good sometimes."

"Oh, thanks," Kallie sulked.

"Well, you get that from me, so I can't point any fingers. It was just an observation."

Kallie laughed, reaching for Sherman again,

who was waiting patiently for his brushing to restart.

"He's your mother's son, you know," her dad reminded her. "He's exactly like her – they might as well be twins. Don't let it get to you."

"It just makes me so mad that she lets him get away with everything. I've never been good enough at anything, but she treats him like the golden child."

"She sees herself in him, Kallie. Flawed and angry," he comforted her. "Neither of them would bother to learn the Jitterbug to dance with an old homeless man, so you should just let them both go."

"I've tried," she joked. "They keep calling me."

Chuckling, he stood up and walked to the kitchen, probably hoping to find one of the ever-present pies.

"Do you know the Jitterbug, Dad?" Kallie called out to him.

"It was before my time, but my mother taught me when I was a kid."

"Grandma liked to dance?" she asked, surprised.

"She was great at it too. And I may have two left feet, but I have a decent memory. If you show me a few steps, I'll probably remember it."

Kallie hummed the song she'd heard in the dance video until she got her rhythm, and then danced a few steps in the living room. She tried to take Sherman for a spin around the room, but he chickened out, jumping up on the couch to escape.

"Sure, I remember that." Her dad returned to the living room, setting down his plate, and nodded his head along with her humming. After a few moments of listening and watching, he started dancing too.

"You really do know it! Let me turn on some music."

She ran to her phone and started a cheerful jazz song, then sashayed back to the living room where her dad bowed gracefully with a grin.

Neither of them noticed the crowd of scheming elderly ladies gathering on the sidewalk outside the brightly lit picture window as they danced and laughed. This time a new face looked out of the crowd and smiled.

* * * * *

"We'd better go," Tess said, finishing her tea and bacon quickly. "Tom's still on vacation and he texted me to ask if we'd open the shelter's kitchen early for the chefs."

"Hang on, I just need to get the spare key," Kallie answered, drinking the last of her coffee and grabbing a diet coke for the road. "I never knew why they left it with me, anyway. I've had it for years and never needed it."

"Okay, but hurry. We need to go."

Kallie ran to the kitchen and pulled open the junk drawer. "It's right in here," she called. "I'll only be a second."

Pulling out the can opener and spatula — *which shouldn't even be in there* — she started digging for the key. "I think it's on a blue keychain." She pulled out a handful of small batteries for the tv and cable box remote controls, D-cell batteries for the hurricane lanterns, C-cell batteries for the Christmas wreath.

"Kallie, hurry! I'm sure someone there has another copy of the key."

A handful of rubber bands, air fresheners, two pens that were obviously out of ink, bamboo chopsticks in old, crumbling paper wrapping. Packets of ketchup and hot sauce.

"Forget it, Kallie. Let's just go!"

"I know it's in this drawer!"

An envelope full of expired coupons, three plastic sporks, a takeout menu from the Thai place up the street, and...

"Found it!"

The keychain was green with pink palm trees, and she ran out of her kitchen with it.

"I found the key," she cheered, holding it up, out of breath. "Let's go."

*　*　*　*　*

"Yum, tortilla soup. My favorite, thank you!" Kallie grinned up at the chef when he brought her a bowl of the day's soup without asking.

The shelter had received a special delivery – several cases of Gatorade and Pop Tarts, which arrived while everyone was eating breakfast. Since there was no room at the tables, Kallie and Tess were sitting on the floor, dividing them up into individual care packages. The heat wave hadn't broken yet, so the electrolytes and extra sugar could literally be a lifesaver.

"I know you two never eat," the chef smiled back at her, handing another bowl to Tess.

"We eat, just not anything healthy. And nothing this delicious."

"You seem like you're coping just fine, but I wanted to let you know — Anna and I are here if you need us." He squeezed Kallie's hand gently. "And *not* just for food." He and his wife Anna owned two famous restaurants in town and were swimming in money, but they were two of the nicest people Kallie knew.

"It was just a scare for me, unlike the poor girl in my car. I'm mostly okay, but thank you so much for thinking of me."

He nodded kindly and went to get more take-out

bags for them to fill.

"So what did that blogger lady say?" Tess asked, when they were alone again.

"Some kids found Alexandra's car down in the everglades, but it looks like someone just took it for a joyride. I'll show you my notes when we get back to the house."

"I'm surprised she's telling you anything."

"Me too. But she's writing a book, and I think I'm basically just her assistant. She doesn't consider me competition or a threat, so basically, I'm just helping her do research."

"You're more than that!"

"Well, yeah. But not to her. And that's fine – I'm not offended. I don't need to make money off of this, or write a book—"

"You just need to get yourself killed by a psychotic murderer." Tess finished Kallie's sentence sarcastically.

"Well, *yeah.* Some people aspire to be doctors or lawyers—" she replied with a wink. "It's just personal, Tess, that's all. I promise, after this is solved, everything will go back to normal."

Without warning, she was swept to her feet and twirled in a surprisingly graceful circle.

"Hi Mack! We missed you last week. Are you okay?"

"Francesca Maria, my dear! My brother and sister came to town, and we had lunch at the Columbia Restaurant. I wish you could have joined us, my darling — it was wonderful!"

Kallie looked down at Tess, who shrugged her shoulders. Mack's family was all deceased, but he definitely looked better this week — healthier and wearing better clothes. He was a dapper old guy, and always dressed neatly — but today he had nearly new pants and was wearing striped blue and yellow dress socks. *Perhaps the elderly widower's late wife still has family who looks out for him?*

"Did you have the paella, Mack?" Kallie asked, playing along with his fantasy. "It's my favorite."

"Mine too, my dear. And they make the best salad."

Kallie had only been to the grand but pricey old local restaurant once, on a date, and wondered if Mack had somehow really dined there lately — or if he and Francesca had visited in their youth. Or maybe it was just a wild figment of his imagination. They did have a famous salad, she knew, named after the year the restaurant had opened.

"Did they buy you the new clothes too? I love those socks; they really suit you."

He stood up and spun around gracefully, belying his age, and danced a few steps. "I like them too." No answer on the clothes, but Kallie could check with the shelter later. *He doesn't live here, but they might know if he'd had a visitor.*

She laughed at herself for planning to solve The Mystery of the Striped Socks, as if there could be some ulterior motive to the arrival of Mack's new footwear. *This murder is making you paranoid, Kalliope.*

But then Mack swept her away and they danced the cha-cha until the subject was forgotten again.

Chapter Nineteen

Kallie was still thinking about Mack's spiffy new socks the next morning. It was probably nothing, and she felt a little guilty for even being suspicious – she should be happy for him, even if it was only a pair of clean socks. They obviously made him feel like a million bucks – she remembered how he had shown them off, and smiled to herself.

Am I being protective or just nosy? Or totally paranoid?

Mack didn't live at the shelter, which was usually reserved for homeless families with school-aged children, but she thought someone there might know the story. They all adored Mack as much as she did, and they tended to watch more closely over their homeless patrons with known cases of dementia. They wouldn't be able to give Kallie any personal information, but she thought they'd tell her if he'd met with Francesca's family members and all was safe and sound. Or if there was someone shady, with an unknown motive, trying to befriend a helpless old man.

Maybe he'd just found the classy new clothes abandoned somewhere, or received them from another local charity. But if he *was* meeting with strangers, she thought the staff would be feeling just as curious and cautious as she was.

Kallie called Beth at the shelter at ten a.m., after she knew the breakfast rush would be over, but got her voicemail. "Hey, Beth, it's Kallie Brooks. I just have a quick question for you. Could you please call me back when you have a minute?"

She hung up after leaving her message and tried to put the whole situation out of her mind. She was running late and needed to get ready for work, and she didn't have the time or energy to worry about anything else right now. She quickly jotted a note for herself, though, to find another swing dance video online, when she got home. She was getting a little rusty and wanted to learn the Charleston.

Showering and dressing in a hurry, she smooched Sherman goodbye and was lucky to hit every green light on her way to work. Her shift had been getting busier and busier as she attracted additional regulars to her section. She'd need to over-stock her section of the bar before the early lunch folks started arriving at eleven a.m., so she didn't run out of anything mid-shift.

I never once ran out of olives or fresh mint when I was working the night shift. Not once! Was it ever this crazy?

But she had to admit, the day shift was growing on her.

Chopping up lemons and limes had always been a cathartic habit for Kallie, a necessary but mindless task that allowed her thoughts to wander. So after her other setup chores were all finished, and her section was fully stocked, she rolled a key lime on the wooden bar counter, pressing hard to loosen up the juice before cutting it. Soon her mind drifted back to the murder, and she wondered again at Alexandra's movements that night. *What was she doing in Odessa after dark, the night she was killed?*

"You sure can wrangle that knife, Kal," a voice beside her observed, making her jump.

"Mike!" After catching her breath, she ran to the end of the bar and hugged him. "I haven't seen you in ages!"

"I'm only here for a minute, but I didn't want to leave without saying hello." His friendly, familiar voice and southern accent were a relief to her ears. "Carlos told me you've been defending my honor."

"It's not funny, Mike," Kallie replied seriously, suddenly frustrated and angry about the whole thing. "The police are really checking you out. They think you might have killed that girl. You need to talk to them."

Mike stopped laughing and sat down at the bar. "Kallie, I've talked to them a dozen times. I didn't know you were really so worked up about this." He looked at her worried expression and frowned. "It's all going to be fine, ok? They'll find the real killer soon, and then everything will go back to normal."

"Talk to Detective Morrison, then. He's the one in charge."

"I *did* talk to him. I told him exactly where I was and what I was doing. But since they can't find me on the camera, and no one remembers seeing me, they can't clear me."

"So where were you?"

"I was outside the back entrance, making my rounds, when a guy came up to me and said that two really drunk girls were walking down Main Street away from the bar. He said he tried to stop them, but they insisted on walking home." He shrugged his shoulders. "You know me, I went after them."

"Of course you did," Kallie sighed.

"I went up the side of the building by the mangroves, and cut through to the street, hoping to catch them before they got hurt – or got picked up by some maniac. I guess I was outside of the camera range, but that wasn't exactly my highest priority at the time."

"Did you catch them?"

"Luckily one of them stopped to puke in the drainage ditch," he replied with a grossed-out face, making Kallie laugh. "They were both crazy drunk. I wouldn't be surprised if they were on some kind of party drug, because none of our bartenders would keep serving someone that drunk."

"You might have saved their lives, Mike. The lighting is terrible on Main Street – if they stumbled into the road, someone could have run them over and never known it."

"That's a little dramatic, Kal. I'm a glorified bouncer, not a superhero. But the address where they were going was over a mile away, so I called them a taxi. That's all."

"Why didn't those girls tell the cops what happened? Did Detective Morrison look for them? I'm sure they'd vouch for you, if they knew."

"They were so hammered, they couldn't have identified their own mothers. If they were even still in town, which is unlikely considering it was Spring Break, I'm sure they wouldn't have remembered me. They probably didn't even remember how they got home."

"I guess," Kallie grumbled in agreement.

"Besides, I didn't kill anyone. So it's all going to be fine. Even that detective doesn't really think I'm the killer, he just can't clear me because I don't have a witness." He grabbed her hands over the bar. "Stop worrying."

"I'll try."

Her friend stood up and walked back around the bar, looking at her with a concerned expression. "I have to get home, but I didn't want to leave without seeing you."

She hugged him tightly and walked him to door. "Thank you for talking to me. I'm glad I finally know the details, even if I have to wait on the cops to fit Owhiro into their busy schedules, before your name is cleared."

"Say hi to your dad and Tess for me."

"I will, and they'll tell you to come over for dinner on your night off – so plan on it."

"Will do." Mike waved and walked away to his car, leaving Kallie feeling a little more relieved.

Until her traitorous, increasingly-confused mind whispered for the first time, *What if he's lying, and he's really the murderer?*

"No way," she mumbled to herself, as she returned to her lime chopping. "I'm not getting *that* paranoid."

* * * * *

Kallie set a frosty pint of beer on the bar for Teddy just as he was joined by Cici and a tall, sandy-blonde stranger. She had never seen them with anyone else before, but after a moment's thought, she guessed he was Cecilia's tequila-toting sibling.

"You must be the brother-in-law."

"Matthew," the newcomer replied, introducing himself with a smile. "My reputation precedes me?"

"You and your magical añejo," Cici answered with a laugh. "Kallie patched us up, the morning after you got here."

"Oh, was that you? I hear you make a mean Bloody Mary."

"That's the rumor," Kallie blushed a little.

"Don't listen to her — it's the best in town, Matthew. And she has a whole arsenal back there, to garnish them however you want."

"That sounds perfect," he began to reply, and then suddenly grabbed his pockets. "I left my phone in the car, Cici. I'll be right back for that Bloody Mary. With, uh, bacon and shrimp?"

Kallie nodded as he hurried back to the door, and soon they saw him dash across the parking lot, almost getting hit by a car. The driver honked angrily, and the two of them quarreled for a minute.

"I don't know how he survived to adulthood," Cecilia sighed. "He gets into accidents and fights everywhere he goes."

"That's funny, he seemed really nice."

"Oh, he's the nicest, most generous guy you could ever meet. That's why it's so weird. Trouble just follows him like a magnet."

"That's why he's flipping houses now," Teddy mentioned. "He got into some trouble on the cruise ship where he worked. We thought he'd stay there until he retired – he loved it, and they all loved him. But something got stolen, and trouble followed him right out the door."

"We know he'd never steal anything," Cici insisted, and Teddy nodded in agreement. "He'd come to us if he needed money, and we wouldn't mind. We even help with the house flipping sometimes. But... well, here we are. Trouble."

Cici stood up and walked away to the window – watching her brother, with her arms clenched nervously across her chest, to make sure he wasn't getting beaten up outside.

Kallie started fixing a Bloody Mary and a Cubanita for the two of them, hoping there wouldn't be a fight outside. A moment later, Josie — who was sitting at a nearby table with her husband, eating a late lunch of cheeseburgers — flagged her down.

"Those drinks look great, Kallie! Could I have one with olives and asparagus? And extra Worcestershire, please. No hot sauce."

"Absolutely!" she replied with a grin.

* * * * *

When Kallie stood up from kneeling behind the bar to collect the various garnishes she needed, Cici had come back from the window and was reaching for one of the drinks. "Matthew just came back in, I'll take this to him," she volunteered.

"Oh, that's not his. That one's for Josie. I already put her olives in it." She added two pickled asparagus spears. "I need to get your brother's cocktail shrimp from the kitchen. We don't keep it at the bar because it's not popular enough. It usually goes bad and starts to stink before anyone orders it," she added with a wrinkle of her nose.

"Oh, I see," Cici replied, looking a little concerned.

"Don't worry, I already entered it in the ordering system, so someone should be back with them in a minute or two." She added Cici's dill pickle to her Cubanita and served it to her at the bar.

Next, she poured a beer for Felix, then added an extra splash of Worcestershire on top of Josie's Bloody Mary and carried both drinks over to their table. Josie took a sip and grinned broadly. "Oh, so good. Thank you!" She pulled the olives out and ate one from the skewer. "You *have* to try one of these," she told her husband.

"Where *is* Matthew?" Kallie heard Cici muttering to herself. "I saw him walking back inside a minute ago." She turned back away from the bar and started toward the window, but abruptly stumbled over her neon turquoise high heels, and crashed into Felix and Josie's table. Their plates and glasses smashed to the floor, and Cici grabbed her ankle and fell clumsily into a chair.

"I'm so SORRY!" she yelped, turning back toward the young couple, who were surveying the damage in stunned silence. "These stupid shoes. I think I twisted my ankle, and I destroyed your drinks and dinner." She looked like she might cry.

Kallie ran over with a roll of paper towels and started cleaning up the huge mess before it spread too far or cut anyone, and a busboy quickly came to help her with a mop and bucket.

"Can I replace their food and drinks, Kallie? I'm so sorry."

"Of course, Cici, but are you feeling okay? How's your ankle?" Kallie replied.

"I just tripped over my own two feet, like a klutz. I'm fine except for a sore ankle and a bruised ego." She apologized to everyone again and then limped over to the bar, assisted by Teddy, as Kallie entered the replacement orders.

* * * * *

"We moved down here from Massachusetts, where we have seasons," Cici mentioned, sipping her ice cold Cubanita. Kallie had explained that this was the real name for a Bloody Mary made with rum, and Cici liked the name so much, she now ordered it regularly.

She had paid for Felix and Josie's dinner and drinks, with even more apologies, and Matthew had finally rejoined them at the bar.

"We have four seasons here too," Kallie replied with a smile, setting down a plate of veggie nachos for them. "Pollen, heat wave, hurricane, and alligator."

Cici snorted a laugh at the local joke. "I sure don't miss shoveling snow, though — or paying someone to shovel snow — and I love the tropical gardening."

"You should see her garden, it's a work of art," Teddy assured Kallie.

"But I really do miss the spring flowers. And the autumn leaves," Cici continued.

"I've always lived here, but my dad has family in upstate New York. We go up there in the fall sometimes."

"We've been here for fifteen years," Cici said.

"Sixteen," Teddy interrupted without glancing away from the Lightning hockey game, which made Kallie smile. Such a quirky couple.

"Sixteen years," Cici corrected herself. "But sometimes it feels like just yesterday we were stuck in the ice and snow."

"You weren't the one shoveling," Teddy reminded her.

"I shoveled occasionally," she told Kallie. "If he was sick. Or pretending to be sick."

Kallie tried to picture Cici shoveling snow in her colorful sundresses, high-heeled sandals, and perfectly-coiffed hair, and failed miserably. But you never knew about people.

* * * * *

"Jack," Kallie growled into the phone, early the next morning. "Ugh, what do you want? And before you ask, I'm broke."

"What? No, I told you I don't need money."

"Then what?"

"It's actually more complicated than that. You know my friend Jason?"

Kallie rolled her eyes. "Friend? Your *drug dealer*, Jason, you mean?"

"Potato, potahto. Look, I owed him some money—"

"I told you—"

"No, listen, I needed an extension on... let's call it a loan—"

"*I hate you, Jack.*"

"And I may have accidentally told him that if he'd give me another week, I'd, um... introduce him to

Tess."

Kallie was stricken senseless, quickly followed by rage. "*What?!*"

"Look, he saw her with you at the beach, and he thinks she's hot. Can I have her number? It's important."

Kallie was still too angry to reply, but she waved her dad over to listen.

"He's not a bad guy, Kal."

"First of all, I'm not introducing my best friend to a deadbeat, sleazy drug dealer. And I know you think this lifestyle makes you seem all troubled and cool, but Tess already hates you. Jason's a wannabe tough guy, but Tess really *will* break your kneecaps."

Kallie looked at her dad, who had his eyes closed with the palms of both hands on his face. If Kallie couldn't fathom that she was somehow related to a revolting idiot like Jack, she couldn't even imagine her father's point of view.

"I'm not bailing you out of a fight with your loser friend, Jack. Introduce him to one of your stupid groupies, and stay away from us."

"Kallie, it's really—"

She hung up on him without another word, mentally exhausted and unsure whether to laugh or scream.

Like I need one more thing to worry about right

now, she thought. Jason was a low-life dirtbag, but not dangerous – still, she'd be sure to tell both Tess and Detective Morrison about the call.

"I'll get Sherman and a diet coke, kiddo," her dad told her, still shaking his head.

Chapter Twenty

Kallie was just setting up her station for the day, when Josie's husband Felix walked in and sat down at the bar.

"Oh! Hi Felix. Wow, I'm not used to seeing you and Josie before your restaurant closes after lunch. I'm not really set up yet," she waved around at the empty bar. Barry was in his usual seat, with a cup of coffee and his notebook, but the rest of the place was deserted. "But can I get you a beer?"

"Can I just get some soup?" he asked.

"Soup? I don't think the kitchen is up and running yet, but I can walk back and check. Are you okay?"

"I just need soup." He seemed dazed, and Kallie stopped setting up the bar to look at him closely, noticing dark circles under his eyes. "I don't know how to make any soup."

"Where's Josie, Felix?" Kallie asked, sensing that something was really wrong. "Shouldn't you guys be setting up your *own* restaurant to open for lunch?"

"She's... Kallie, she's sick. We went to the emergency room, and she's really sick. We just live down the street, and I know you're supposed to give sick people soup."

It wasn't normal for him to babble.

"Okay, you're starting to worry me, Felix. Is it the flu?"

He chuckled in a weird tone that made Kallie's stomach lurch. She walked around the bar and sat next to him.

"She threw up and then fainted. And she was shaking. I had to carry her to the car. She had to stay overnight in the hospital and get an IV, but they said it's just a bad stomach bug and sent her home."

His hands were shaking too, but Kallie didn't think he was sick. She thought it was panic setting in.

"Okay, Felix, I don't think you should be here," she said slowly, like she was speaking to a child. "Go home and stay with Josie, and maybe just order delivery. It doesn't sound like she should be alone." She started walking him toward the door. "If she gets any worse, you take her back to the hospital. They'll help you."

"I'll bring you the soup, Felix," an unfamiliar voice called out to them.

Kallie looked around and saw Barry walking toward them. "Place the order with the kitchen, and I'll bring it down to your house when it's ready."

She had never seen him speak to anyone but her

before, and even that was rare.

"Are you sure?" Felix asked.

"Sure. You should order something for yourself too. When was the last time you ate?"

Felix laughed awkwardly and waved off the question, but Kallie was pretty sure she heard his stomach growl. "I'll take a chicken quesadilla, then. Plus the soup." He scribbled down their address, which was barely a block away – then paid and left quickly, wanting to get back home to Josie.

"Thanks, Barry. That was really nice," Kallie told him when they were alone again.

"It's no problem. They're in my book, you know," he held up his notebook and tapped the cover. "So it's the least I can do."

So that's what he's always writing...

"You're in it, too," he called back over his shoulder as he returned to his usual seat.

"Yikes. I'll make sure to be on my best behavior, then," she smiled, still surprised at the random kindness of strangers.

* * * * *

After work, the stress of the day wore on Kallie, and she couldn't focus on anything at home. She tried reading as a distraction, then watching a silly show on television, but nothing worked. And she couldn't get Hannah's surveillance photo out of her head.

Everyone says Lex was a homebody, not a party girl – a recent transplant, and not someone with a lot of friends in the area. So what was she doing eighty miles from home, in the dark, on the night she was murdered?

After trying to watch a movie or play solitaire on her phone, and failing miserably to get the thought out of her head, she finally gave up. Knowing Tess would yell at her for even suggesting it – and insisting to herself that a grocery store parking lot couldn't be dangerous – she took off for Pasco County alone.

Half an hour later, she pulled into the shopping center in Odessa where Alexandra's Audi was last believed to have been seen. She had no idea what she expected to find, since the photo had been taken several weeks earlier, and the parking lot had already been searched – but she wanted to at least look around.

Kallie's heart beat a little faster as she reached the section where the Audi had been parked. *Lex was right here, so close to her death. I can almost feel her pointing me in the right direction.*

And then she opened her own car door, and the feeling fled instantly. It was just a dirty, smelly strip mall, like any other parking lot in the world. Maybe smellier than most, due to the lack of rain.

Not giving up, Kallie walked around the location, bending to look closely for anything that might give her a clue of why Lex had stopped here. An oil leak, broken glass, maybe a single drop of blood? *Does a flat tire leave any kind of mark*, she wondered?

But there was nothing in the area where the car had been photographed, except a sticky spilled milkshake and an empty bag of baby carrots. She was ready to give up and go home, when a familiar voice spoke behind her.

"Now, why am I not surprised to see you here?"

Kallie yelped and whipped around, startled by the voice, and nearly stumbled into him.

"*Detective!* What are you doing here?"

"Apparently the same thing you are," he replied with a smile. He was dressed in jeans and a striped button-down shirt and was barely recognizable. "This is out of my jurisdiction. And I trust my colleagues up here, but I still wanted to check it out for myself. Off the clock."

"I saw the photo of the car online," Kallie explained her presence, stretching the truth a little. "So you think it was Alexandra's car too?"

"It's a pretty clear photo, but the license plate isn't visible." He seemed to be considering how much he could tell her. "I think it's likely, though, yes. Audis aren't that common. Since it was later found abandoned, and the interior of her car was compromised, I hoped there might be some evidence left here."

"I didn't see anything," Kallie replied, immediately realizing how dumb that sounded. "I mean, not like I would be qualified..."

"I know what you meant, Miss Brooks. And I know you wouldn't have *touched* anything if you did find evidence—"

She shook her head no, trying not to look guilty, and looked down at her feet with the wild hope that a clue would appear on the grimy asphalt. She was about to say goodnight, when she suddenly realized this was the perfect opportunity to go back and check out the houses in Devotion. Hopefully *also* the crazy homeowner. This time with a protector.

"Hey, listen, Detective" she tried to sound casual. "Those plots of land aren't too far from here. Could we drive out there and check them out? I know you can't, like, investigate. But if you're not too busy..."

"You have the addresses?"

Kallie fumbled in her purse for the notepad, and handed it over to Morrison, looking up at him expectantly, holding her breath.

"This isn't too far away. Maybe twenty minutes." He thought for a moment, looking like he wanted to back out, but apparently he was as committed as he promised. "Fine, let's go."

"What is this in your trunk?" Kallie called to Morrison as she stuffed her large purse and duffle bag into the back of his car. She had changed out of her good shoes, slipping on the Converse she kept in her car – in case they needed to walk around the two large lots. "Can I move it?"

"The bag? It's part of my hurricane kit."

Kallie held it up in the light and saw that it contained a bottle of iodine tablets, a small battery-powered LED lantern, and a half pint of vodka.

"This is *it?*"

"No, I have a full storm kit at the house. This is just stuff I might need in the car, if I have to help other people before I get home. There's a basic first aid kit back there somewhere too."

"Of course you'd think of helping other people first. My hurricane kit has, like, potato chips, batteries, and five bottles of diet coke. And forty pounds of dog food and six gallons of bottled water for my dog."

"Naturally," he laughed.

She slid Morrison's belongings over enough to add her own bags in the trunk, and then climbed into the passenger seat. "We would evacuate anyway, though. Even if it's just to a pet-friendly hotel, further inland. Don't you?"

"Nah, they need the cops here for the storm aftermath, so almost all of us stay in town. But there's room for us to stay at the police station – it's like Fort Knox."

"Oh, I guess I forgot."

"Forgot I'm a cop?" he asked with a crooked smile.

"Well, I mean, you're not a normal cop. You're a detective. Doesn't that give you a pass to evacuate?"

"Probably, but I don't want a pass," he replied with a shrug. "And like I said, it's safe."

Kallie nodded, not really surprised.

* * * * *

After watching the rural scenery pass for a few minutes, Kallie repeated the question that had been bothering her for weeks.

"So does this mean you don't think it's Mike anymore?" Kallie asked, looking over at Morrison in the driver's seat.

"I really can't talk about it, Miss Brooks. I think this lead in Devotion is worth checking out, but I really can't discuss other aspects of the case." He looked over at her for a moment, then added, "I'm sorry."

"What about the runaway landlord and his lousy alibi?"

"Oh, that was actually straightened out," he replied with a barely audible sigh of relief. Kallie knew this could be a long drive if she kept pestering him, but she couldn't help it. "Keaton just mixed up the dates. He thought he was at the pizza place on Saturday night, but it was actually Friday night."

"Does that clear him?" Kallie asked, feeling mixed-up.

"Yeah, he was on the restaurant's cameras on Friday night. He was actually bowling at Nice Pins on Saturday evening, and there were half a dozen reliable witnesses who verified it. Apparently he's a pretty dramatic bowler. Not good, but... memorable."

"Wait, so you can tell me *this* part, but not about Mike?" she asked, confused and trying not to get annoyed at what seemed like hypocrisy.

"Those details were actually released to the press, but no one wants to print the *boring* news about innocent people," he grumbled.

Kallie noticed the bitter tone of his voice and was a little surprised – it seemed unlike him. Wanting to clear the air, she asked, "So you think this idea might be something?"

"There's no way of knowing until we get there. We knew about the arts center she was trying to build, but I don't think anyone found the location, since

Pasco's not in our jurisdiction. Nobody has time to drive up here during work hours." He glanced over at her with a nod, which she took as a compliment. "We can only wait for them to send their findings, and they don't have much spare time for cases in our jurisdiction either. It's tough. But especially now that we know her car was up here on the night she died, it's definitely worth checking."

"There's no sensible reason for her to have been up here at night."

"We don't know that, though. Keep in mind, we barely know anything about Alexandra Clemons. I know it's easy to feel like you know her personally – and I've had that exact same feeling with other victims, believe me. But she could've had a million reasons to be up here, unrelated to these houses."

"Like?" Kallie asked, a little more sarcastically than she intended.

"Scouting other properties?" Morrison suggested. "Visiting her real estate lawyer? Shopping at the outlet mall? Seeing a secret boyfriend? Hiking? Sightseeing? Maybe she just likes driving?"

"Okay, okay. I get it." Kallie sulked a little at his logical reasoning.

"For all we know, she could have been up here visiting the giraffes," he added, and they both laughed, imagining Lex visiting the popular but rustic local safari ranch in her designer suits and heels.

"Anyway, maybe there'll be another surveillance camera along the way, if nothing else. They're everywhere now, and that would be a huge help."

* * * * *

"Morrison," Kallie said after they'd been driving for a short time. She saw nothing but trees around them. "The GPS on your car just went out. Can you get the directions on your phone?"

"What? Oh, sure," he answered. "We're getting pretty close, but I'm not sure where to go after the exit. Hang on." He put his phone in a hands-free holder and opened an app, preparing to look up the directions, but he wasn't getting a signal. "We must be out of range of any cell towers."

"What should we do?"

"We'll just keep driving. We had another ten miles to go before the exit, I think. I'm sure we'll reach another tower before then, and they'll reset."

He started digging through the glove compartment and then peering into the back seat. "I think I have an old map in here somewhere."

"A what? Like an old-fashioned paper map?"

"I bought a map book of central Florida when I moved here. A spiral bound book. It's old, so the trendy streets in downtown Tampa will all be wrong, but these old side roads and highway exits in the country never change. It's in here somewhere."

They drove another ten minutes without the GPS or a signal. "Maybe there's a cellular outage. Help me look for the map."

"You're serious? Okay, you're serious." Kallie climbed awkwardly over the center console and into the back seat. "You said it's a spiral-bound book, right? Not just folded paper?"

"That's right," he called back, still fiddling with the GPS to no avail.

"Well, it's not back here." She climbed over the rear seats, into the hatchback trunk area. Pulling back a few beach towels, she raised her hands in victory. "Found it!"

"Excellent! You can navigate," he suggested. Kallie climbed back into the passenger seat with the yellowed, tattered old book. "Oh, do you know how to read it?"

"You've met my dad, Morrison. Does he seem like the kind of guy who wouldn't teach his daughter to read a map?"

"That's a fair point," he conceded. He reached over and flipped the book open to the first few pages, which each showed a whole county, covered in a grid of rectangles. There was one page for each of the seven counties in the Tampa Bay area. "Show me."

She flipped to the Pasco County page. "We're on highway 54, which is this line," Kallie ran her finger across the page, "and we just crossed route 589, so we're in *this* box." She poked a rectangle marked "23", and then turned to page twenty-three.

"Awesome. Just making sure."

"Except the map doesn't have exact addresses, and I don't remember how to get there."

"Oh. Right. We'll worry about that when we get closer."

* * * * *

"I used to think my parents were crazy and paranoid," Kallie told Morrison, mostly to fill the silence of the drive. "My mother made me lock all of my car doors when I was driving the two miles back to my dorm in college. My father wanted me to carry a gun. Not just in my car, but in my purse."

"It can be a dangerous world."

"Sure, but not around here. Certainly not in Owhiro. And not enough to live in fear all the time."

"But now you think they were right?" Morrison asked, sounding genuinely curious.

"Maybe," Kallie reflected.

"Are you afraid all the time now?"

She nodded, surprised at herself, confiding secrets that she hadn't even fully confessed to her best friend. "Even in my own house. I don't even want to take a bubble bath or sit on the lanai alone."

"That will wear off, in time," Morrison told her. "I promise. If the memory of fear stayed glued to you like that, our ancestors would never have left their caves. And women would certainly never have more than one baby!"

She nodded. "You sound like you're speaking from experience. How long does it take?"

"That depends on you. Don't try to rush it. But *do* try not to think about it. Watch movies that make you laugh. Listen to music that makes you dance. It helps."

"You sound like a psychiatrist."

"You remember that serial killer? He was caught in my sister's neighborhood, barely a block from her house." Kallie gasped and clasped her hand over her mouth, remembering how he had gunned down pedestrians completely at random, night after night. "It wasn't like what you went through — I mean, she's fine. But I saw a therapist a few times."

"Really?"

"This job, you know... I can handle the threat to my *own* safety. But I wasn't ready for that. And we basically have a shrink on the payroll at the police station now," he added with a laugh. "It wasn't like that until recently. No more Mister Tough Guy cops, these days. Anyway, it took me a few weeks to stop constantly worrying about her, obsessing that it could have been her – and trying to convince her to buy an alarm system. And a gun. And a rottweiler." He glanced over at Kallie, unsure of whether to go on. "One night, I slept in my car outside her house," he added, blushing a little.

She was surprised that he would confide this much in her, too.

"But we can't live like that," he added with an air of finality. "She was fine, and you'll be fine."

"It just doesn't— Hey, I think that's the house."

"Perfect. Let's go."

Chapter Twenty-One

As Morrison was getting out of the car, Kallie pulled him back.

"Um, I need to tell you something first. This guy might not be completely stable."

The detective looked confused. "You know him?"

"When Tess and I were up here at the deed recorder's office, we decided to drive out here, just to look around. Since it was so close."

"Miss Brooks—" he sighed.

"We didn't even go on the property!" she exclaimed before he could yell at her. "But this guy saw me on the sidewalk and freaked out."

"Why didn't you tell me this sooner?"

"I knew you'd be mad at me. But Morrison, he *really* scared me."

He shook his head and took the addresses from her. "I'd rather not go in there without knowing if he's dangerous, but I can't try to find his identity without a cell signal. Our patrol cars have a dedicated signal, but out here, in my personal car, I need my phone. Even then, it would just be googling, but I'm pretty good at it. Your phone isn't working either?"

Kallie held up her phone – no bars.

"And you don't have his name?"

"Oh, let me think..." *It was on the paperwork. Think, Kallie.* "Wait, I have a photo of one of them, and I don't need a cell signal for that." She scrolled to the photo of Lex's refrigerator and showed him the handwritten note.

"I'm not even going to ask why you have a photo of Alexandra's refrigerator," he muttered.

"Oh, uh, yeah. Let's roll right past that. This is the wrong house, anyway. The other house belongs to C&W Trust. I saw the deed for this one, though. I think the guy's name was... Jackson?"

"Okay, that's not *really* helpful," Morrison replied with a wry smile, "but at least—"

As Morrison was speaking, the door of the house opened, and Kallie immediately recognized the wiry, unpleasant-looking man who walked out on the porch. He looked around into the darkness, obviously suspecting he was being watched.

"Great," Morrison whispered, turning to Kallie. "I know this guy. He's got a reputation all over the bay area. His name's Johnny Jackson, and you're right, he's dangerous. Stay here."

Kallie considered arguing, but if the detective

was actually worried about her safety, instead of making fun of her, it was probably for a very good reason.

"Who's out there?" the man called from the back porch, when he heard the car door opening. There was a single light bulb above his head, but the car and yard were shrouded in darkness.

"Hey, Johnny. It's Detective Morrison." He walked toward the house with his hands visible.

"Morrison? You can't bother me out here. It's harassment or somethin'."

"This isn't about Brenda, Johnny. I just want to ask about one of your neighbors. You know the folks around here?"

"Nah, not many of 'em," Johnny answered. "Not like when I was a kid, and we all knew each other."

"Yeah, me neither," Morrison answered with a shrug, walking closer to the porch. "Nobody does anymore." When he got close enough to stand in the light from the porch, he held up the photo of Lex. "You ever seen this girl?"

The sinister-looking man backed cautiously toward the door but squinted at the photo. "Sure, she's been all over the TV. Pretty kid. I never seen her around here, though."

"Never? Not even visiting any of your neighbors?"

"Like I said, I don't know 'em."

"But you see them, right? See folks coming and going from work. Driving, shopping at the gas station on the corner, walking their dogs."

"I mind my own business, Morrison."

"Yeah," the detective nodded, apparently certain that much was true. "Sure you do. Thanks for your time."

Just as he had given up, something struck the man on the porch. "Can I see that picture?"

"What? Yeah, sure." He walked closer and handed over the worn out, folded printout of the girl who had been seen on every television in the country.

"I might've seen her out here, a month or so ago. Asked me if I wanted to sell my house."

"Did she offer you money?"

"Sure, and said she'd pay me twice what it was worth. She didn't look like this picture, though. She was wearin' a fancy suit and high heels, but I recognize her eyes. She was drivin' a real fancy car, but she wasn't stuck up. Didn't talk to me like I was stupid. She seemed like a nice kid."

"I've heard that before. Did you agree to sell the house?"

"She said she needed to talk to someone else, but she'd bring back a contract. I never saw her again."

"Okay, well thanks, Johnny. I appreciate the

help."

Jackson nodded and walked back into the house without another word.

* * * * *

"No dice?" Kallie asked, when Morrison got back in the car.

"Nothing helpful at the moment."

"Why did he want to see the picture of Lex?" she asked.

"He said she offered to buy his house, but he only saw her one time."

"At least we know we're in the right place. Can we go to the other house? It's pretty close."

"We might as well."

Morrison put the car in gear and drove to the next driveway, which was half a mile up the bumpy road. Unlike Jackson's house, this place was on the edge of the woods, and the house was surrounded by a tall, concrete block wall.

"Anything you want to tell me about this place, before we get out? Maybe it's owned by a killer clown who tried to—" A loud bang interrupted the detective, making them both jump.

"Was that a gunshot?" Kallie hissed, sitting up

straight in her seat.

Morrison reached for his personal revolver slowly. "I don't think so. It was probably a car backfiring on the highway. It didn't sound loud enough to be a gunshot."

Kallie glanced down at the gun in his hand. So did he.

"Yeah, I'm going to check it out anyway. Stay here."

When he stepped out of the car, though, she was right there with him. "I'm not staying in this creepy forest alone, Morrison."

"You think a vampire's going to get you?"

"Vampire, alligator, grumpy mama bear. Chupacabra. Nothing good lives in the forest, especially in Florida."

"Fine," he sighed. "But stay behind me."

"Do you think this is the murderer's house, Morrison?" she whispered.

He was silent for a second, and then simply answered, "Probably not."

Kallie stayed behind him, as ordered, but clung tightly to the back of his shirt with one hand.

"That's not exactly what I meant. Can you let go of my shirt, please?" She shook her head no, and he smiled. "I pictured you running in there like Mad Max, Miss Brooks."

"I did too. So we were both wrong."

They walked awkwardly up to an ornate metal door in the surrounding wall and Morrison knocked, announcing himself, but no one answered. He tried the doorknob, but it was locked.

Kallie reached out from behind him and tried the doorknob a second time, then looked up at him and shook her head. "Locked."

"Yes, I got that, thanks."

"Does that mean we have to go back, now?"

"Well I don't have a warrant, so we don't have much choice."

"But the gunshot?"

"It didn't sound loud enough or close enough to have been a gunshot. But it does give me a little leeway to look around."

"You should see the old ladies snooping around my house, Morrison. Surely we can at least look for blood in the yard, right? We know Lex was in this area on the night she died."

"Do you think you can climb up there?" he pointed at the surrounding wall – eight feet of concrete block covered in flaking stucco.

"No."

"If I lift you, can you just *look* to see if there's enough room on top to sit? We need to see what's on the other side."

241

Kallie lifted an eyebrow. "Still no."

"Okay, I'll do it. Maybe I can stand on the car. " He started to walk back to his car, which was the only thing nearby that was strong enough to hold his weight.

"Forget it, I'll do it."

"Are you sure?"

"Do you promise to take me to the chiropractor in the morning?"

Morrison laughed. "I promise." He crouched down and made a step with his hands, where she could put her foot for leverage. Then he nearly launched her over the wall.

"MORRISON!" she yelped, clawing at the wall for traction.

"I'm so sorry! I thought you'd be heavier."

"WAS THAT SUPPOSED TO MAKE ME FEEL BETTER?"

He blushed like a schoolgirl and tried awkwardly to explain. "Sorry, I'm used to picking up men."

She raised an eyebrow. "Maybe you should quit talking while you're ahead." She couldn't help laughing at his discomfort, though she was still hoping he hadn't just called her fat.

"I mean, we practice this at work, and in the military, and it's always with men. I misjudged how much lighter you'd be."

"That sounds a little better," she replied with a suspicious squint down at him as she leaned on the top of the wall.

"Are you okay? Are you balanced up there?"

"I can see into the yard, but it's too dark to make anything out. I need a flashlight or something."

Morrison handed her his flashlight, and she took it carefully, to avoid losing her balance. Leaning on her elbows, she pointed the light into the darkness, and was shocked by how bright it was. It lit up the entire side yard, all the way to the house.

"Whoa," she whispered.

"What? What is it?"

"It's *beautiful*. Wow, it's like the Garden of Eden, or Sunken Gardens or something." After her initial shock, she looked around the yard a little more. "There are a bunch of holes dug in the yard, like someone was planting recently, but I don't see any lights on indoors."

"Can you get down on that side?"

"Are you *crazy?!*"

"If you hang by your fingers and drop, it won't be that far."

"I'm gonna hang *you* by your fingers, if you don't get me down from here, Morrison. Like *now*."

The detective helped Kallie down carefully, and followed his previous plan of climbing over himself, using his car for support. Soon he had landed on the inside of the surrounding wall and cautiously opened the outside door to let her walk through.

At eye level, Kallie found that the yard was horribly overgrown, but it was covered in masses of colorful flowers and shrubs. A wave of jasmine fragrance blew through her hair as she stared around at gardenias, bougainvilleas, and blooming hibiscus in a dozen different glorious colors and sizes. Plumerias and crepe myrtles towered over her head. It looked like a magical garden – probably haunted, or at least bewitched – from a fairy tale.

They checked out a few of the recently dug holes, but there was no sign of planting, and no shovel. Morrison didn't want to surprise the homeowners if they were inside, so he approached the house carefully and knocked loudly again.

No reply, but this time the doorknob turned easily in his hand.

Chapter Twenty-Two

"Are you sure this place is empty?" Kallie whispered as she followed Morrison into the dark house.

"No, Miss Brooks. I know exactly as much about this place as you do. Unless there's more you haven't told me?" He stopped and stood silently, listening.

"Is anyone home?" the detective suddenly yelled, making Kallie jump. "I'm with the St Petersburg police, and we thought we heard gunshots. Is everyone okay?"

Kallie punched him in the arm for scaring her, and then they both stood quietly motionless again.

"So either it's empty, or they're planning to ambush us."

"Great," Kallie whispered, grabbing the back of Morrison's shirt again. She felt his shoulders slump in what she presumed was resigned annoyance, but she didn't let go.

The detective turned on his flashlight again, which lit up the small house even more brilliantly than the garden. Kallie immediately wished he'd left it dark, as the huge taxidermied head of a wild boar loomed inches from her face. Its eerie glass eyes and vicious-looking tusks made her cringe against Morrison's back even harder. Turning her face away, she found a stuffed bobcat fixed in mid-pounce on her other side, shiny fangs glistening in the flashlight's glow.

"Can we please pick another room," she hissed at the detective, who seemed unfazed by the horrible relics.

"You know, if you'd let go of me, you could go anywhere you'd like," he suggested, but then obliged her request, leading her into the kitchen.

How can that beautiful garden and these creep-tastic dead animals belong to the same person? Or would that be normal for a psycho killer?

Kallie was stunned to find that the kitchen was completely normal. No stewing eyeballs, no bones hanging from the walls. Not even a lowly bottle of arsenic.

Salt and pepper shakers sat next to the electric stove, and she opened the cabinets to find simple blue plates and matching glasses. Kallie's eyebrows arched in surprise, and her grip on Morrison's shirt loosened a little.

As they turned down the hallway toward the bedrooms and single bathroom, the detective called out again, "Is anyone here? Is anyone injured?"

Silence.

Kallie saw him shrug as he kept walking, but when he turned into the first bedroom, he stopped short.

"What?"

"I don't think you're going to like this one, Miss Brooks."

"More dead animals?"

"Not exactly."

Kallie peeked around the corner and saw a whole wall full of eyes glowing back at her. Some of them were winking. She let out a low groan in her throat and backed away.

"They're just dolls..."

"That's fine," she replied, leaning against the wall with her eyes closed, taking deep breaths. "I'll take the other bedroom."

"Do you really think the other bedroom is going to be any better?" the detective laughed.

"Probably not," she whispered, but kept walking.

But it was. The second bedroom was as uncharacteristically normal as the plain, ordinary kitchen. It didn't appear to be a guest room and had obvious personal touches – but it could have been found in any suburban home.

Morrison caught up with her, looking over her shoulder into the room.

"Nobody shot, and no sign of the attack on Alexandra Clemons," he concluded. "I'm afraid I've outstayed my reasonable grounds for entry, Miss Brooks. We should go."

Morrison turned back toward the door, obviously hoping she'd follow, but Kallie lingered to check the bathroom. Impatient but visibly reluctant to leave her alone, even though the place seemed deserted, he walked into the second bedroom. Looking out through the window, hoping to see the newly dug holes in the yard, his line of sight was blocked by a gigantic bush with pretty pink flowers and long, narrow leaves. Like the rest of the plants, it was completely overgrown, but even the detective apparently thought it was pretty.

"That's an oleander," Kallie pointed out. "My grandmother loved them, but I wasn't allowed near them in her garden because they're poisonous. Seems silly to have it covering the windows, when they already have that giant wall for privacy." Resisting his signals that they should leave, she went back to inspecting the bookshelves.

Morrison gave up on trying to rush her and walked back down the hallway to wait in the kitchen.

The whole place was cluttered with piles of clothes, and boxes and bags of belongings, but it didn't seem dirty. *Maybe they had agreed to sell the place after all, and had started packing*, Kallie thought. *Or maybe they were just amateur hoarders.*

There wasn't any record of a sale, even a pending one, and Kallie couldn't imagine trying to sell a weird place like this. *But if Lex was going to tear it down, she wouldn't care about the downright creepy decor.*

She was walking back to the kitchen, under the glassy gaze of the stuffed boar's head, when she heard someone in the living room.

"Morrison?" she whispered, slipping around the corner into the dark kitchen.

Silence.

"Crap. Morrison? Is that you?"

He'd been in the kitchen a minute ago, but now he was gone, and she could hear the sound getting closer. She crept up and peeked around the corner, hidden behind the piles of junk and clothes, but she couldn't see into the living room. She knew she didn't want to meet the creepy homeowner, especially by surprise.

I should've waited by the car, like Morrison told me to do. Now that crazy man in the living room is going to hear me, and turn me into one of these dusty, taxidermied relics. Run!

But where was Morrison? What if he was in trouble? Even worse, what if he was in trouble because *she* hadn't waited by the car? What if her distracting him caused him to be captured or hurt?

Guilt lurched into Kallie's stomach, overwhelming her fear. She took off her shoes and tiptoed back to where she'd last seen the detective, begging her feet not to step on a loose, creaking board — or anything sharp. As she reached the first bedroom, strong arms grabbed her, and a huge hand clamped over her mouth.

"Don't make a sound, Brooks," Morrison hissed quietly in her ear. She slumped against his chest in relief, but he didn't remove his hand from her mouth.

"There must be another way out of here." His voice was barely louder than a breath, and he started to pull her toward the door when a huge raccoon came bounding out of the living room, making a scurrying racket as it ran down the hallway. Kallie shrieked as it scampered past her, and she ran for the door, dropping the shoes she was still carrying. The creature was well-fed and nearly Sherman's size, but it seemed oblivious to her yelling.

Morrison was trying hard not to laugh, and he graciously collected her shoes while she continued her beeline for the exit.

The flashlight's glow lit up the living room at the opposite end of the hallway. It looked like an old-fashioned parlor, with long couches and tiny, spindly end tables. Its former grandeur had all had fallen to rags and dust, beneath the stare of an incongruous giant moose head.

Kallie's heart was pounding wildly, and she was ready to run for the hills, when something caught her eye. There was a large old framed photograph on the wall that grabbed her attention, and she took it down to look closer. Even in gaudy 1970s clothing and bad haircuts, she immediately recognized the two teenagers grinning up at the camera from a picnic table. She shook her head in confusion and carried the picture back toward the kitchen, where the glow from the flashlight was brighter.

No mistake.

"How can that be?" she mumbled to herself, slumping into a chair and wondering if she was dreaming. Even without any new evidence, she was convinced that this was the killer's house. She closed her eyes, confused and exhausted, but determined to figure out why the murderer would have *this* picture. Was he planning his next killing?

She stood up and walked to the front window, still stewing in her thoughts, staring absently, but another of the silly, huge pink oleanders blocked her view. She laughed at herself for forgetting it was there, turning away – and then a scowl creased her forehead.

She walked back over the table, sat down, and picked up the photo again. She looked at the picture for a moment, closed her eyes, and took a deep breath, concentrating. *Think, Kalliope! Why is this here?!*

Suddenly her head snapped up and she

screamed for Morrison.

Chapter Twenty-Three

"We have to get back to Owhiro, fast," Kallie grabbed Morrison's hand as she pulled him toward the door, with the framed photo still in her other hand. "I know who killed Alexandra."

"Wait, what?" the detective pulled up short, inadvertently yanking her to a stop. "Didn't you think the people who own this house killed her?"

"They did, Morrison. But they aren't here. Come on. I'll explain on the way."

* * * * *

Teddy McNally answered the door, smiling charmingly at Detective Morrison and his colleague.

"Hello, officers. Can I help you?"

"Good evening. We actually need to speak with your wife. Could we come in?"

"Of course! Forgive me, please come in. I'll get Cecelia."

Once Detective Morrison and his accompanying officer – who had met them at the corner – had entered the home, Kallie quietly joined them, staying near the door. Teddy looked at her strangely but smiled and gave her a little wave as he went to retrieve Cici.

The glamourous blonde stopped at the doorway, a look of surprise on her face. Even wearing casual evening clothes, she looked splendid in a colorful, flowing kaftan and sparkling pink flipflops. She quickly recovered from her confusion with an apologetic look. "Oh, my. Are you here to see my brother, Matthew? I'm afraid he isn't here at the moment."

"Actually, Mrs. McNally, we wanted to speak with you."

"Oh, okay. Please, have a seat," she replied, taking a seat herself on an overstuffed chair. She was eating from a box of Swedish Fish and offered them to Kallie. "Did you know they're vegan?"

Kallie shook her head silently, knowing she'd never be able to eat them again.

"We have some questions about the Owhiro murder. Can you please tell us where you were that afternoon and evening?"

"We weren't even in the—" Teddy started to reply, but Morrison cut him off.

"Please, sir, we'd like to hear it from your wife."

"We were at the Lazy Gecko in the afternoon," she replied. "But Matthew and I needed to meet someone about a house we're flipping. Teddy wanted to stay a little longer, so we took my brother's car."

"And where is this house?" Morrison asked. "The house that you're renovating? Flipping?"

"It's north of here, up in Devotion, Florida," she replied.

Kallie sighed and slumped against the living room wall, closing her eyes.

"Could you tell us the exact address?"

Cici rattled off the address of their fixer-upper, which Kallie already recognized as the address where she'd found the photo.

"And what happened that day, at the meeting?"

"Nothing special, we were just scheduled to meet with a tile specialist. He was going to replace the kitchen backsplash for us. It was a quick meeting, but he wanted to see the location because it's a custom tile."

"But hadn't the house already been purchased by Alexandra Clemons?"

Cici's face paled a little. "No... no, we were still negotiating."

"So you admit that you're the owners of the C & W Trust?"

"Yes, Cecelia and William. My brother's first name is William. Matthew is his middle name, but he's always preferred it."

"And using his middle name made his criminal

background less likely to be discovered?" Morrison asked. Cecilia didn't reply, but looked down at her hands, gathered in her lap. "What happened, Cecelia? If you didn't want to accept her offer, couldn't you have just declined?"

Silence.

"She might have made you a better offer. Or she could have found another plot of land," Morrison continued.

Silence. Teddy was looking back and forth between Kallie and his wife, confused but quiet.

"It wasn't worth her life."

Cici kept her eyes down, rubbing her hands together for another moment, as if trying to wash them clean. "That's not what happened," she finally whispered.

They all sat silently, waiting.

"Those charges against Matthew from the cruise ship?" she mumbled, staring at her glamorous sandals. "They were all true. He stole about fifty thousand dollars' worth of jewelry, but they could never prove it. He buried it all in the yard just after we bought the house, in case the inspectors came to find him."

Morrison waited patiently for Cici to continue, while Kallie listened in shock.

"Alexandra's offer was too good to pass up, and we decided to sell. I was digging up the stolen jewelry, so Alexandra's workmen wouldn't find it when they tore down the house."

Kallie knew what was coming next, and she held her breath.

"She snuck up on me," Cici moaned. "We must have left the outer door open. I didn't even hear her, and then she touched my shoulder and scared me half to death. Before I knew it—"

Morrison was nodding patiently, sympathetically, for her to continue.

"Before I knew what happened, I was standing over her, with the shovel still in my hands…"

Kallie closed her eyes again and covered her face, and Teddy looked like he might faint. Tears slid down his cheeks.

"I didn't know what to do. I went inside and got Matthew and pulled him back outside to see what'd happened. I was doing it all for *him*, so I thought he'd help me."

"But he refused?"

She shook her head. "Not right away. Alexandra was wearing an unmistakable emerald green Chanel suit and matching heels, and he pointed out that we needed to fix that. He helped me get her into some old clothes from the shed and move the body into his car – but then he changed his mind and wanted to go to the police. I told him we couldn't – that they'd find out about the jewelry, and we'd *both* go to prison." She looked up at the detectives with a frown of resignation. "We drove both cars back to Odessa, and then went to the Lazy Gecko to find Teddy, but he'd already left. We must've left the doors open too long, because the battery in Matthew's car died."

She looked at Kallie, who was staring at her in shocked sadness. "I never meant to hurt you, Kallie. We needed to have the car jump-started, so we couldn't leave her body in there. We just picked the nearest car, which happened to be yours."

The room was silent for a moment while they all considered this awful coincidence.

"Matthew still insisted that we go to the police. He nagged me about it constantly, every day – saying he couldn't sleep, couldn't eat, couldn't stand it anymore. And he eventually told me that he was going to report me."

"Did he?" Morrison asked.

Cici seemed not to have heard the question, staring at her hands again. "He *betrayed* me. After all I did for him. I was trying to protect him, my baby brother, and he was going to turn me in for... an accident. It was an *accident!*"

Morrison shook his head dismissively, but Kallie had already realized one more thing.

"You were going to poison him," she whispered, barely audible. "At the Lazy Gecko, with the Bloody

Mary. You were going to kill your own brother."

Cici nodded almost imperceptibly.

"But it was Josie's drink. That's why you knocked over their table."

"I didn't know what else to do," she groaned. "I was afraid she'd die too."

"She almost did." Kallie remembered the look on Felix's face when he'd come to get the soup for Josie – how scared he was. "And the poison was from the pink oleander in the yard?" Kallie guessed.

Kallie's blonde, vivacious, funny friend – now an admitted murderer – nodded again.

Chapter Twenty-Four

Tess swept through the front door just as Kallie was sticking a spoon into a pint of mint chocolate chip ice cream. She was in her pajamas and her eyes were still red from crying.

"Your dad called me," Tess explained as she dropped onto the couch next to her best friend and caught her in a tight hug. "Why didn't you tell me what happened? I would've been here sooner."

"I don't want to talk about it," she sniffled.

"We don't need to talk, honey." Tess called Sherman over to the couch and he hopped up on the other side of his mistress, snuggling against her.

They sat in silence for a while, until Kallie's anger finally overwhelmed her grief and lingering sense of guilt. "I can't believe I trusted her. I actually *liked* her."

"She fooled everyone. Even the police. If you hadn't found that old picture of Cecelia and her brother, and realized that was the house they were flipping, she might have gotten away with it."

"You know, everything was already over before I even met them. The murder and cover-up had already happened. Even the blonde woman in Lex's Audi, in that picture, that was Cecelia. I'm so mad at myself for not seeing it, when she was right in my face almost every day. And I'm even more mad at *her!*"

Tess didn't bother replying, she just hugged Kallie and let her vent.

"I can't believe she tried to kill her brother in *my* bar, with *my* Bloody Mary!" She fumed. "And almost killed an innocent bystander in the process."

"With *your* world-famous, mind-blowing, award-winning, best Bloody Mary in all of central Florida," Tess replied, very seriously, finally drawing a laugh from Kallie.

"I'm just so mad that I liked her, Tess."

"I know, honey. And I'm so glad you're the one that caught her."

"Me too."

The trio sat in silence for a few more minutes, as Kallie sniffled and took solace in her best friend and her awesome dog. "Can I have some of your ice cream?" Tess finally asked.

"I got your favorite, butter pecan. Go get it out of the freezer so we can talk, ok?"

Epilogue

"Excuse me," a woman's voice behind Kallie called as she and Sherman returned from their walk a few days later. She mentally prepared herself for battle as she spun around.

But it was a woman she'd never seen before. No high heels, no garish lipstick. And no pie.

"Hi, I'm Anna. I live up the street." Her silvery hair was in a high ponytail, and she wore jeans and a black t-shirt. Her black tennis shoes had pink laces. Kallie liked her immediately.

"I noticed the commotion when you and your father were swing dancing last week. I wondered if the two of you might like to join us at the Blue Heron Club this weekend? We're starting a dance club on Sunday afternoons."

"That sounds fun, actually. I'm not much of a dancer, I've just been practicing a little. But my father's really—" she turned toward the house to gesture, but her dad was already standing at the top of the stairs, smiling.

"Dad, this is Anna," she called to him. "She's starting a dancing club that sounds like exactly your cup of tea."

She left them chatting on the lawn, like two old friends, remembering what Tess said about her dad meeting the right lady.

* * * * *

Once the murder was officially solved, the story disappeared from the television news cycle pretty quickly. Kallie and Tess had heard enough about the Owhiro Murder to last a lifetime, so they didn't miss it.

Hannah still mentioned the murder occasionally, texting Kallie to tell her when the book was finished, and when she sold it to a publisher. She gave Kallie major credit and offered her an investigative writing spot on the blog any time she wanted it.

Finally, when Tess, Kallie, and her dad were working on a new jigsaw puzzle one night, a story on the news caught their attention. Alexandra's dad was on the screen, for the first time in ages, and he was joined by Lex's colleague, Penny Jameson.

Kallie turned up the sound on the television just as Mr. Clemons was saying, "I've researched my daughter's plans and location choices for the arts center that she wanted to build." He took Penny's hand for a moment. "I've decided to fully fund the 'Alexandra Clemons Center for the Performing and Visual Arts' in

Devotion, Florida."

Kallie's living room burst into cheers and happy tears as the camera cut to a professional plaque with the center's name and Lex's photo. Her dream would finally come true after all.

* * * * *

"Nobody ever takes Memorial Day seriously," Morrison mused, looking at the upcoming holiday ads for booze and burgers. He had offered to take Kallie to lunch in Clearwater as an unofficial salute to her hard work. The sheriff's office was working on an *official* commendation, she'd heard, and she was dreading that idea. "It's not just a day for grilling and drinking beer and sitting by the pool."

"Well, it's sort of like the unofficial start of summer," she replied with a shrug. "In places where it hasn't already been summer for four months, I mean."

"I guess."

"My dad and I go to a morning memorial service down in St Pete every year. You're welcome to come with us."

"Really?"

"Sure. Fair warning, though – we usually get barbecue takeout and sit on the beach at Fort DeSoto afterward. There might be beer."

"I suppose that might be okay," Morrison replied with a laugh. "As long as it's *after.*"

"So you were in the military? Before you were a cop?"

"Yeah, straight out of school. I don't really talk about it."

"That's fine, my dad doesn't talk about it either. You two tough guys can *not-talk* about it together. Like Fight Club or something."

"Like two dudes."

"Exactly," she laughed. "Two dudes. Your secret's safe with me. Anyway, we leave early. You can meet us at the house around seven, or just meet us there if you want."

"I'll meet you at the house. I can drive, if you want to ride in a car with a working rearview mirror."

"Lavish! That sounds like a plan. See you then."

"Sure. And hey, thanks."

* * * * *

Books by Tanya Westlake:

Bloody Mary, Bloody Murder

Piña Colada Calamity

Mai Tai Malice